THE MIRROR FROM THE ATTIC

JOEY HOFFMAN

Order this book online at www.trafford.com
or email orders@trafford.com

Most Trafford titles are also available at major online book retailers.

Printed in the United States of America.

ISBN: 978-1-4907-1361-8 (sc)
ISBN: 978-1-4907-1360-1 (e)

Trafford rev. 09/04/2013

 www.trafford.com

North America & international
toll-free: 1 888 232 4444 (USA & Canada)
fax: 812 355 4082

TO MY READERS,

THANK YOU FOR choosing to read THE MIRROR FROM THE ATTIC. It is my hope that you will enjoy the storylines of Matt and Dominique, Wrek and Nisa, and the four boys as they encounter adventure and heartache through a mysterious mirror.

Writing fictional stories about my family is a dream come true for me. It is fun, but also hard work. There are days when I want to pull my hair right out of my head, but then an idea or the next words arrive, and I'm off and writing again.

I thank my Lord and Saviour, Jesus Christ, for without the blessing of the talent he instilled within me, this book would not of been possible.

Look for my first novel, THE GREEDY COURIER, as well as my third novel THE BOUNTY HUNTERS to be released in late 2011.

Happy reading!

Joey Hoffman

CONTENTS

ONE

THE DEATH OF STANLEY

THE DOOR SLAMMED shut. Dominique advanced and opened the unscathed structure. She watched Matt stagger down the staircase to their basement bedroom as he stressed his opinion about her kids.

"You're wrong about them," she yelled as she tailed after him. "They don't walk all over me."

"Yes, they do," he slurred as he stopped at the bottom of the staircase and looked up. His face bore weariness. "Nick quit school and he sits around the house doing nothing."

"He does favors and chores for me and . . . Why do you care so much anyways, I'm the one supporting him."

He gazed at her with bloodshot eyes then took a drink of beer before exiting the situation. "I want an annulment!"

"So do I!" She turned and stomped upstairs, her cast redden with anger. It had been a month since their wedding and she couldn't believe the unfavorable comments that had just been spoken. She understood his words to be the alcohol talking, but was it his true feelings emerging to the surface?

She lit a cigarette and stepped out onto the lighten porch. Darkness had fallen and through the distant streetlights, she could see Nick riding his bicycle toward their house.

"Hi Mom," he greeted when he neared and bumped his tire into the step. He had beads of sweat about his forehead that had dampened the edge of his bangs.

"Matt's in a grumpy mood. He told me he didn't want to be married anymore."

Nick thought for a moment as he took hold of his sleeve and wiped his brow. "Is he packing his bags?"

"I don't know, but if this is how he's going to act, I'll pack his bags for him."

"Good mom."

The next morning, Dominique was helping her youngest son, Ian, dress himself for soccer when Matt arose from the basement. Without speaking a word to his new family, he walked to the refrigerator, grabbed a pop, and bypassed them as he headed toward the bathroom.

"What was that?" Dominique questioned as she sat in awe.

"Is he mad Mamma?" Ian's expression held a hint of curiosity.

"Something. I'll have to talk to him after the game." She strapped on his second shin guard. "The game That you're gonna win for me." She lifted her gaze to meet his and smiled.

"I'm going to kick a goal for you and a goal for Andrew."

"Your daddy would be proud."

"What about me?" Travis teased. His straight blond hair lined the base of his white taut face. "Are you going to kick a goal for me?"

Ian put his finger to his rugged chin. "Okay."

Later, Dominique and her three tired boys returned home from gaining victory on the field. Travis and Nathan's team had no relief players today while Ian earned his three points. Her heart sank when she noticed Matt's car was absent from its space. After entering into her house, she went downstairs to her bedroom to see his clothes and belongings still in their place.

"Mom?" Nathan shouted from the top of the staircase, "Can Sandy come over?" Nathan was a husky fellow whose brown hair was shaven to a buzz and his eyes were a curious mix of brown and mischief.

"After I make lunch." She really wasn't pleased about his new friend. Sandy was two years older and more aware of the mature things of the world. She was going to keep a close eye on them.

The afternoon moved in slow motion while the television emitted entertainment and Dominique wrote on her fiction. Nathan, Sandy, and Ian were upstairs creating race cars out of legos while Nick and Travis rode their bikes around Kellogg.

Matt arrived home and after entering into the house, he sat on the couch. He was unshaven and burdened with heavy thought.

Dominique spun around on her desk chair to look at him. She waited for conversation and even though she felt angered by his lack of attention, she took into her sight, his handsome face and medium build.

A few moments later, Matt spoke. "My dad died."

She turned away from her thoughts. "Well I know his death doesn't bother you much, right?"

"Yea."

"How's your mom doing?"

"She's okay."

"When did he die?"

"He was passed on when my mom awoke this morning." He took in a deep breath and ran a hand through his thick hair. "She was expecting it though. We were all expecting it."

"Yea." She stood and walked over to join him on the sofa.

"The funeral will be early next week."

They discussed his father's death briefly. Soon there was a break in their conversation so Dominique asked him if he remembered what he had said last night.

He looked puzzled. "Be more specific."

"The annulment?" She bit her cheek.

He groaned in protest. "I don't remember."

"Well I do," she changed the tone of her voice. "It sounds like you should quit drinking."

He gave her a look of disapproval.

"You shouldn't give me a dirty look," she pitched, "You know what I've been through with Andrew—his abuse." She stood and went for her cigarettes. "I thought you wanted to have a different kind of relationship than what you had before with Michele? No lies, no fighting? Think about who's the common denominator in all this."

He felt a little guilty and didn't want to argue. "You're right." He arose and signaled her to near him. He wrapped one arm around her waist and soon his body began to react to her nearness. With his free hand, he reached to the back of her head and ran his virile hand through her long hair. He looked into her eyes. "Don't you know I love you and I want to be with you forever?"

"Ditto," she replied, then kissed him.

Nick walked through the living room. "Yuck!" he remarked because of their affection.

Matt leaned in close to her ear and whispered. "You want to go downstairs?"

"Why?" she asked with seduction in her voice. "What are you going to do to me?"

"Follow me and you'll find out woman." He took her by the wrist and led the way.

Ten minutes later, Dominique and Matt were interrupted by someone banging on their bedroom door. "Mom?" She heard Nick's call through the wooden structure.

"What the heck is going on?" she spoke her wonder to Matt as she jumped out of bed, then tossed her clothes on and ran up the steps where she unlocked and opened the door. "What's wrong?" she asked.

"There's a cop here."

"Oh no," she exhaled through her breath. While she walked to the front door, she recalled the last time she had spoken to a cop; A cop who notified her of Andrew's death.

"Hello, are you Travis Kerr's mom?"

"Yes," she answered with fear.

"Your son fell at the swimming pool and he was taken to the hospital by a volunteer."

She began to worry while Matt stepped up behind her and put his comforting hand atop of her shoulder.

The plump officer spoke. "He injured his leg."

"How bad?"

"Probably just a bruise . . . the worst," he assumed, "A hairline fracture."

She turned and looked straight at Matt. "Ian? He was tired of playing legos so I let Travis take him for a swim."

"He's in my car," the officer spoke.

They followed the policeman to his car where he let the boy out.

"Travis broke his leg Mommy."

"I know sweety." She bent down and hugged him.

Matt wanted to help. "I'll go get you car keys," he informed his wife as he turned and raced for the house.

Daylight was declining when Dominique arrived home with her wounded son. While she carried his crutches and medication, Matt and Nick helped Travis into the house and to his bed.

"What's on his leg?" Ian asked.

"It's a cast."

He reached forward and touched it. "It's hard."

The day of the funeral was hot and sunny. Matt sat on the pew in between his wife and mother Jasmine, who wore a black permanent press pant suit. He was sporting a brown western suit that brought the dark tone of his skin about. By his natural features, he would guess he was part Indian.

The atmosphere of the service wasn't of gloom or melancholy, for his adopted father was known for having a strict hand. Of course Jasmine loved her husband and graciously forgave him of some of his wrong doings. However, she would still miss him.

Matt turned his attention to Dominique who matched his western fashion. "I'll be right back." He stood to his feet and inched his way to the aisle.

After he visited the restroom, he was slacken in the foyer when he saw the funeral director open the casket. He felt sick to his stomach as the thought entered his mind of seeing his father's face one last time.

As he stepped through the aisle toward his seat, he gulped down his feelings and pushed the thought away, for he had to be strong for his family's sake.

The sermon was short and an eulogy from a friend brought wonderful memories for some. Matt and his brother, David, stepped with their mother to the casket. Jasmine touched her fingertips to her late husband's cold lips while Matt cast his vision to the flowers. He felt a sudden blast of coldness sweep across his face, causing his hair to sway. He instantly looked at his mother to see if her gray hair was wavering. When he saw the stillness, a chill ran within his spine.

TWO

MOVING TO A NEW HOUSE

DOMINIQUE'S SMILE COULDN'T grow any broader after talking to her agent, Dorothy Lee, over the telephone. Her first novel was going to be published.

Dominique was a petite woman with a figure that could drive a man crazy. Her long golden hair flew backwards as she ran up the staircase to express her joy to her sons.

"We're going to be rich!" Travis cheered as he jumped on his one sound leg.

"Yes," she agreed, "But we're still going to pray and obey the Lord."

Matt laid his hard hat on the passenger seat after he sat and stuck the key into the ignition. His black hair was plastered to his skull and his hazel eyes shifted about as he backed out of a parking space. He rolled the window down and soon, the breeze had blow-dried his hair into a fluff.

It was Friday and Matt was ready for the weekend. The month had flown by with good news about his wife's advanced pay from her book sales, a much different week than the week before when his father had died and was put to rest. As he drove down the road, he lit a cigarette and gave thought to the day many years ago when he first set eyes upon his new home in Northern Idaho, in Smelterville. He was barely five when his adoptive parents brought him home. He recalled his father's tall and sturdy frame and the tonic he wore within his black hair, his mother's smile that blended well with her soft skin and curly brown hair. He shed a half grin when he remembered the Micky Mouse watch his dad had given to him.

Matt quickly left memory lane when he heard sirens and had to hasten out of their way.

Dominique was putting books into a box when Matt entered through the door. She turned and observed his merry appearance. "You're home!" She looked at the time. "It's five o'clock already?"

As he stepped to the bookshelf, she arose and then he kissed her. "Did you get the keys today?"

"Sure did. I also changed our address and called the utility companies." She set the last book into the box. "You want to go get the moving truck?"

"Let me take a fast shower." He darted away.

"Wrek's here," she shouted.

Minutes later, Matt returned from the basement shower dressed in his blue jeans and white Nike high-tops. He went into the kitchen. "Hey," he greeted Wrek who was standing at the counter beside his duffel bag. He turned to Dominique. "Is Nick around to help?"

"No, he's working for the carnival this weekend, so you'll have to settle with Wrek's help."

"That's all right. I'd rather see him earning a few bucks for himself."

Dominique grabbed her cigarettes and wallet, then cast her eyes to Wrek. "We'll match you a bowl when we get back." She followed Matt out the door.

The next afternoon, Matt and Wrek had the furniture and large boxes loaded onto the truck. Wrek was breaking down the trampoline when Ian pushed his bicycle up to him. "Don't forget my bike," he said.

"I'm going to take those training wheels off," he poked fun as he observed the seriousness on his nephew's face.

"No, Uncle Wrek, I'm not ready for that yet." The young boy quickly steered his bike away from his uncle. He maneuvered it toward the fence and through the open gate where he left it beside the moving truck.

Travis wasn't much help. Aided by crutches, he felt like an unnecessary bystander, but he liked it. He just observed the removing and loading when he wasn't playing his video games.

Matt drove the large truck to their newly purchased house while Dominique and her gang followed in the car. She parked on the side of the road and Matt backed in.

"This is great!" she bragged of her house after she keyed the lock and entered. She knew her oak furnishings would compound well within the spacious living room. The floor yielded blue carpeting while the walls were a slight gray. The brick fireplace was painted white and a large bay window gave view to the grassy front yard. A staircase had been installed at the center wall that led to the smaller bedrooms and a large water room.

Ian ran through the empty house. "I get the big bedroom," he shouted, "It has a bathroom."

"No you don't you little whippersnapper," Dominique replied, "That's my room!"

"And Matt's?" he questioned.

They reviewed the house. Matt stepped into the master bedroom and admired the mirror walls in the west corner. His nasty thoughts of Dominique temporarily surfaced before he glanced at the yellow walls and knew they had to go. The yellow reminded him of the dull mustard color that was on his childhood bedroom walls. He also recalled the cheap wooden bunk beds and the seventies style plastic chairs that he would always set his watch and school books on.

Further into his memories, being a three and a half foot boy, he remembered when Stanley walked into his room and with a strict voice, he laid down the rules. He was in a stupor as he looked upward into the face of the scary giant who meant what he said.

Dominique came into the room.

Matt pushed the thought away and turned to her. "I'm going to the paint store."

She smiled broadly, showing her teeth. "I knew you'd want a different color. I want a black cherry color." They walked into the kitchen and to the counter where Wrek was breaking a nugget from a large bud and sticking it into his pipe. After a few tokes, Matt left in their car to go buy the paint.

Some thirty minutes later, Wrek carried into the house, a large box. He set it on the floor and as he panted, he rolled to his butt. "Break time."

Ian came dashing through the open door. "Mommy?" he called out, "Nathan took my soccer ball."

"He probably wants you to help carry things in."

"I am," he stressed.

"In between kicks?" she spoke with humor.

Wrek took a drag from his cigarette. "Is soccer season over with for the year?"

"Yea. The boys played their last game Saturday and tomorrow is Ian's trophy party. Want to come with us?"

"Sure, but what about Nathan and Travis? Do they get trophies?"

"They received ribbons." She raised her eyebrows as she turned and looked at her brother. "I was surprised when Travis got one, he only played a half season."

There was silence for a few moments. Dominique pulled a brush out from her purse and began to stream it through her hair. Her zircon bracelet swayed from her tiny wrist.

"You're lucky Dom," Wrek said in a downcast voice as he dabbed the cherry of his cigarette into the ashtray.

"Why do you say that?" She observed the drooping of his head.

He lifted his head. "You have a family. I have no one."

"You'll meet that special someone, someday," she sympathized with him.

"Someday? I'll be old by then. My peter won't even want to work anymore."

She chuckled.

He glanced her way and accompanied in the laughter.

"Well," she hesitated, "I know one thing that might help."

"What?"

"Brush your teeth."

"Ha ha."

"I'm serious Wreker. When was the last time you brushed your teeth?"

"Two . . . years ago . . . I think."

The following week was a busy one for Dominique with the cleaning of the rental unit as well as the fashioning of her new house, talking and planning with her agent, and shopping for school clothes.

It was mid-morning and she was sitting at the kitchen table when Matt approached her. "What are you doing?" he asked after he observed her cutting on her sons' new school clothes.

"I'm cutting off the gee gee's."

He expressed a puzzled look. "What the hell is a gee gee?"

She laughed as she turned her head and looked up at him. "The tags."

"O . . . kay." He leaned down and kissed her. "Will you be ready by two?"

"Yea, I'll go with you to your mom's for dinner."

THREE

A CHILLING ENCOUNTER

AFTER DINNER, MATT went outside and took hold of a ladder. He set the tip of it onto the side of his mother's house and gazed up at the small door. He, nor David, had ever been allowed up there; it was their father's attic.

He crept up the ladder and keyed the padlock from the latch. He pushed open the squeaky door, peeked in, and reached for the switch. When the light came on, he beheld the cob webs that were scattered amongst the dusty old junk. There were antique gadgets hanging on the walls and pieces of smaller furniture covered with sheets and cloth.

It was an eerie feeling for him as he stepped in on the creaky wood floor. He was barely able to stand; his hair brushed against the ceiling. His curiosity arose as he ducked and shifted himself about. The dust stirred, he sneezed. He then made his way around until he came upon a trunk. He sneezed again and again as he knelt and unlatched it.

Dominique stood at the door with a flashlight. "Your mom finally found it in the kitchen cupboard."

"Come here!" He glanced at her. "There's a chest over here." He grabbed the edge of a nearby sheet and blew his nose. "Is David coming up?"

"He's behind me," she spoke as she stepped in.

David was plump in the gut so he stopped on a step that allowed his head to be a foot above the base of the door. He scanned the proximate space. "Anything interesting back there?" he shouted.

While Dominique aimed the light upon the latch, Matt lifted the lid. They saw a few photographs lying atop of linen. He picked up one of the framed pictures and studied the face. He wondered why his dad would have a photo of a little Indian girl.

"Matt?" David called out.

Dominique stepped into David's view and informed him of the chest.

"What else is in the attic?"

"Just a few plastic chairs, boxes. Stuff covered with sheets." She returned to Matt.

"Look what I found," he whispered to his wife as he displayed a large rock from his palm.

Her eyes widened. "Wow!" Is that real?"

"It sure is." He put his finger to his lips. "Don't tell anyone about this gold."

While he stood, she took a glimpse of the interior of the chest and saw a small sized pair of beaded moccasins and a silver necklace.

Matt slipped the rock into his jeans pocket and set the lid of the chest to the rim. He stepped around and lifted a few sheets to see a dresser and a mirror. "Come look at this mirror Dom," he suggested.

She eyed the full length reflector. "This is a pretty cool mirror," she commented before she reached out to caress the mahogany frame that was supported upon two long feet. She took note of the claws that were centered by screws located on the two vertical columns. She gently pushed the swing mirror backwards. "Awesome."

Matt returned the glass structure to an upright position. "I'll ask my mom about this mirror." When he pulled his hand away from the edge of the glass, he saw his thumbprint.

He leaned in and closely eyed it. "Huh?" he spoke with bewilderment as he watched his fingermark vanish into the glass. He turned and looked at Dominique. "Did you see that?"

There was silence.

"Never mind," he said when he sensed she saw nothing. "I guess it was Just the lighting." He covered the mirror and led the way to the open door and down the ladder.

He lit a cigarette and walked into his mom's house while Dominique stayed outside with the kids. After ten minutes in the house, he joined his wife at the swing set. She was pushing Ian. "My mom said we could have that mirror," he told her, "It belonged to my dad's old girlfriend."

"Did you know about her?" she asked as they stepped away from the play area.

"No. I was kind of surprised when she told me. I guess she was an Indian."

"That would explain the moccasins, huh?"

The following Saturday, after arriving home, Nathan visited the restroom before walking into the kitchen where his mom was. He greeted her with a hello.

"What have you been doing all afternoon?" she asked as she sliced a tomato in two.

"Hiking in the mountains with Sandy."

She stopped dicing the fruit and turned her frown towards him. "That's dangerous. How far did you hike up?"

"Sandy took his two machetes with us," he rationalized as he displayed sympathetic eyes.

"I don't like it, it scares me."

"I'll be okay Mom."

"Would one of those machetes really protect you from a hungry bear or mountain lion?"

"I think so. One slice across the throat and he'll be down." He poured himself some orange juice.

"One swipe with their claws and YOU'LL be down."

The smell of dinner was adrift when Matt arrived home from his mother's house. He carried in the cloth wrapped cheval and set it in the center of the living room. "Where do you want me to put this?" he called out to Dominique.

"Set it in the laundry room for now."

The boys were dressed for bed and watching tv when Dominique took a bucket filled with warm water and dishsoap into the laundry room. She set it on the floor next to the glass cleaner and mirror, then tossed a washcloth onto the rim of the pail. She stepped to the speculum and gathered the cloth. As she began to unveil the antique piece of furniture, Wrek and Nick entered into the room.

"Awesome piece of glass," Nick remarked.

Wrek lit a joint and passed it.

When Dominique sprayed the cleaner onto the glass, the overruns became the color of brown. She mopped the surface with several paper towels before a glow was apparent.

She took hold of a dry towel and reached upward to carefully clear the years of dullness from the top. As she wiped, she saw small bits of reflective material fall within the air and disappear. She turned to Wrek. "Where did you buy that pot? I just saw green sparkles!"

"No way, not from pot," he argued.

She directed herself back around and wiped again. All she attained this time was, the fine, dry particles of dust.

The next day, after enjoying the potluck at church, the Jax family arrived home to relax for the day. Matt slid a movie into the VCR for the family while Ian hung about in his bedroom.

When the movie ended, the older boys headed out to the backyard. Nick practiced his archery while Nathan watched from the trampoline.

"The bulls eye Nick," Nathan hollered, "not the straw."

Nick, with blue eyes and waves of brown hair, was a strapping young lad whose life goal was to become a mechanic or bounty hunter. At age sixteen, his frame had already taken shape to that of a muscular man and he was sporting a full chest of hair.

Dominique walked through the hallway and stopped at the laundry room door when she saw her brother. "What are you doing? I thought you were going to lounge all day?"

"I forgot that I needed to wash my clothes."

She stepped into view of the mirror and gave attention to her physique. "I like this large mirror," she told Wrek, "I'm keeping it."

She exited the room and decided to check on her clan out in the back yard. Ian was jumping alone on the taut canvas. "Where's your brothers?"

"In the garage. Mommy, watch this!" He jumped high and presented to her, a front flip.

"Good job!" She continued to the garage door. She could hear her sons talking and when she reached for the knob, she heard Nathan speaking of a cave he and Sandy explored. She stayed quiet and listened.

"We stepped slowly through the ankle deep water," he bragged, "until we heard a growl."

Nick's eyebrows went up.

"Then we got the hell out of there."

Dominique pushed open the door and glared at her son who had shock erupting from his face. "You're grounded!" she yelled, "Grounded until I get back home from my book tour!"

FOUR

BEYOND EXPLANATIONS

IT WAS THE last weekend of summer and the first of the leaves were turning color. Dominique and her household were enjoying an afternoon of tubing up the North Fork, especially Travis who no longer wore a cast.

As she drove home, the rain followed. "It looks like we won't be barbecuing," she said after glancing upward at the clouds.

"Maybe it will let up soon," Travis suggested from the passenger seat as he combed his wet hair.

Soon enough, she was parking under the awning when Matt pulled in behind her with his new truck. They exited the vehicles. "I'll unload the inner tubes later," Matt called out while everybody rushed to the front door.

Twilight was in. Travis and Nathan were upstairs in their bedrooms deciding what new items to wear tomorrow for the first day of school while Dominique and Wrek quickly cleaned the dinner mess. "It'll be nice to have a break from the dishes," she told her brother.

"Lucky dog. I still wish I could go with you."

"I need you here Wrek."

"I know," he replied sadly, "Matt can't take care of four boys."

"He doesn't know how to be a father," she added.

Nick entered the kitchen. "You got that right."

Dominique turned toward him. "But everyone's going to be nice and get along while I'm gone."

"I will for you Mom."

"Thank you." She set the wet washrag upon the sink's divider and turned off the light. "Kitchen's closed," she said as Wrek hung his dishcloth and followed her into the living room.

She stood by the door and smoked before sitting on the couch. Ian climbed onto her lap. "How many more days until you leave, Mommy?"

"Two." She held him close and kissed the top of his head. "Are you going to miss me?"

The day after tomorrow arrived. Matt offloaded Travis and Nathan at school before driving his wife to Spokane to catch the train. He drove into the lot and halted in a parking space.

"I'm scared Matt."

He looked at her. "Scared of what? Signing your autograph, meeting your fans?"

"Yea," she spoke softly as she leaned aside and rested her head upon his upper arm.

"You just don't want to go alone."

"I wish you were going with me."

"I thought you wanted me to stay home and watch over the house and make sure Wrek was taking care of the boys?"

"I do and I don't."

Some ten minutes later and Matt was waving good bye to his wife as the train pulled away. "Hurry back woman," he spoke under his breath.

Evening had come. Matt was wiping the coffee table of oddments when the telephone rang. "Hello," he answered.

A heavy, but familiar voice emitted through.

"Dash! When did you get out?"

Wrek and Nick carried in a bench from the back porch and placed it in the laundry room against the wall.

Matt soon hung up the phone and followed to see what his brother-in-law and stepson were doing. "Why are you putting that in here?" he asked from the doorway.

"Stoner's bench," Wrek replied.

"Well, let's try it out." He stepped forward and sat.

Wrek lit a joint and passed it to his nephew.

"Where's Ian?" Nick questioned his uncle.

"He's in his bedroom watching TV."

Matt took his toke. "Those kids are so spoiled," he complained, "A TV and VCR in each of their bedrooms."

"Don't forget Nathan and Travis' new video game systems," Wrek added.

"I never had a TV in my room when I was younger."

"Times have changed."

"And I'm going to get a car!" Nick bragged as he raised his arms in cheer.

"That's bullshit," Matt grumbled.

"Why?" Nick asked, "How does it hurt you if I get a car?"

He was silent as he inhaled his second toke.

The room was filling with smoke. Wrek clamped the roach clips onto the half smoked joint and toked.

"Look at the air by the mirror," Nick proposed, "Doesn't the haze look green?"

"Yea it does," Matt agreed as he arose to his feet. "It looks like a layer from the ozone."

"I think the ozone is blue."

"Blue, green. Same thing," he spoke as he stepped forward and slowly moved his arm through the colored air. "Awesome!"

Wrek and Nick chuckled. "You look like a mime."

Without warning, Matt was sucked through the glass of the full length mirror. Wrek and Nick turned their heads toward each other with open jaws and beheld the situation.

"What the hell?" Wrek stood to his feet and Nick followed. "How can he just disappear like that?" he asked as he peeked behind the mirror.

"Don't ask me, I'm just as surprised as you."

Wrek reached out.

"Wait! What are you doing?" Nick gasped in panic.

"I'm going where Matt went to." With his fingertips, he touched the cheval glass and in a flash, he was swallowed up from Nick's sight.

Nick shrugged his shoulders and touched the reflector. "Ahh . . ." he uttered as he departed through the framed structure.

After arriving to an unknown location, Nick scanned the area in hopes of reuniting with his uncle and stepdad. As he stood alone upon a sidewalk, he took notice of the high-rise buildings, the traffic lights, and the few palm trees that were alined around a lush lawn. He observed an American flag hanging from a building; it was positioned next to another flag that had a blue base with red and yellow rays emitting from a center copper star. "I'm in Arizona!" He stepped to the intersection and read the street sign. "Central Avenue."

"Nick?"

He turned toward the call. "Matt, Wrek. Thank God," he said as they approached him. "I think we're in Arizona."

"Phoenix," Matt confirmed, "But why, I wonder?"

"You tell us," Wrek urged, "It's your mirror."

"Maybe," Nick suggested, "We're not really here, we're just walking around as ghosts."

"Like an illusion?" Wrek asked as he pulled a cigarette from his pack.

"Yea."

Wrek kicked him in the butt. "Was that an illusion?"

Ian exited from his bedroom. "Uncle Wrek," he called out as he walked into the kitchen. "Uncle Wrek, I'm thirsty." The small boy went to the refrigerator and tried to open it. He held onto the handle and placed his feet upon the door, then tugged. From his weight, the door opened. He fell to his rear, then arose and grabbed the gallon of chocolate milk. He set the container on the table and climbed the counter for a glass. After returning to the floor, he poured the chocolate milk into the glass until it gushed beyond the limit of the rim. "Uncle Wrek? Help me," he yelled.

Matt, Wrek, and Nick ambled upon the sidewalk along Central Avenue. There were few passersby, for most of the city dwellers had gone home for the day.

"That's an awesome looking tall building," Nick commented as he gazed upward.

"Come on," Matt instructed, "We need to find a phone and call Travis." He glanced around the vicinity.

"And tell him we're in Arizona?" Wrek turned his eyes to his brother-in-law. "He ain't going to believe us."

"Maybe not, but someone needs to watch Ian."

He agreed.

After walking a block, Matt spotted a building that resembled a Mexican restaurant. As they were crossing an inlet to an alleyway, a scream caught their attention. They came to a halt and observed a rough-looking man who was forcing a small woman into the cab of a truck.

"I think she's being kidnapped," Wrek theorized as he inched his way into the alley.

"Damn it!" Matt complained as he followed.

While the fellow ran around the front of his truck, the three spectators ducked behind a dumpster. "We need to save her," Wrek urged.

"How?"

They heard the engine start. Wrek who was the most determined, took off running and leaped onto the ladder of the camper. As the truck sped up, he held on tightly and turned his head around to Matt and Nick. "Follow me!" he yelled.

FIVE

IN PURSUIT

WITH GREAT HASTE, Matt and Nick ran through the alleyway after the speeding truck. They watched the vehicle as it turned left.

Wrek finished climbing the ladder and laid atop of the camper. He pressed his feet tightly against the ladder bars and with his hands, held onto the side rails. "Don't fall off," he told himself as he saw from his side view, different objects flashing by.

The two runners halted at the border of the alley and noted the camper truck becoming smaller with distance. "How are we suppose to follow him?" Nick asked as he gasped for air.

"We need to find a vehicle with a key in it."

They hurried through the parking lot of the restaurant, checking ignitions of the parked vehicles.

"This one," Matt quickly spoke, "Get in and don't leave your fingerprints!" He pulled his long sleeves over his hands and opened the door of the compact auto. He turned the key and sped upon the one-way street.

"I can't believe we're stealing a car," Nick remarked.

"We're not. I am."

They traveled south on First Avenue to the intersection of Central Avenue. "I hope we're going the right way."

The traffic light shifted to green and Matt pressed on the accelerator. They blended within as the traffic rolled forward under a freeway overpass and across a bridge.

"I think I see him."

While they followed at a distance through a residential area, Matt recalled the last time he raced through the streets in a stolen vehicle. He was sixteen and had been drinking when he became angry with his father. He had taken possession of his father's truck without his permission and went joyriding through an open field, damaging a few fences and destroying mailboxes. At least this time, he thought, there were no squad cars in pursuit of him.

"He's turning right," Nick exclaimed.

Matt refocused in on their quest and directed the borrowed car into the turning lane. "Dobbins Road," he imprinted into his mind.

The camper truck veered into a private driveway and traveled the half mile gravel lane until it disappeared behind a shabby blue house.

Matt remained out of sight through the dust trail, then he parked off to the side of the roadway amongst a few tall Paloverdes. He and Nick exited the car and kept to the protection of the trees and bushes as they snuck closer to the stranger's house. "Watch out for rattlesnakes," Matt warned.

Wrek released his grip when the truck slowed and came to a stop. He straddled backwards onto the ladder and jumped to the ground as the engine was deactivated.

The abductor opened his door and as he forced his prisoner out, Wrek heard her pleading for him to release her. Wrek peeked around the corner of the camper and saw that the rampageous stranger had a pistol. He pulled back. "Damn it!" he lipped. Wrek was a small man who didn't much like violence. He knew he wasn't brave enough to just step out and attack; to take his weapon and prisoner with quick tactics as a superhero or ninja would do.

Matt and Nick stood before the outermost tree and studied the surroundings. There was a span of fifty yards or so between them and the dwelling place. "I bet they're in that house."

They knelt and concealed their cigarettes as they contemplated on their next move. "Should we wait until dark?" Nick looked to Matt for an answer, but instead, he saw, within their proximity, green air, followed by flashes. "I think we're going to be . . ."

After a few moments, they were standing in the laundry room in front of the full length mirror.

"That was awesome!" Nick boasted.

"Tingly," Matt replied as he viewed his hands.

"Where's Wrek?" They turned and as they looked at the glass, he swiftly emerged through and bumped into them, knocking them to the floor.

They composed themselves. "Did you follow me?" Wrek asked.

"We did."

"We have to go back," he urged. "He might kill her!"

"Okay, but wait, we need to check on Ian." His thoughts were rapid. "And grab some things to help us."

They hastened out of the linen room. Wrek went to Ian's bedroom. "Ian?" he called out as he peeked in.

Matt walked into the kitchen and noticed a puddle on the floor. "It looks like someone spilled the chocolate milk," he spoke to Nick before he glanced up at the clock. "We've been gone for an hour and a half."

Wrek sprang up the staircase to Travis' bedroom. He knocked lightly and opened the door. "Is Ian in here?" He looked within the expanse.

"Where were you guys?" A soft voice came from under the bed as he popped his head out.

"Did you go outside?"

"No," he replied.

"We were in the garage." He turned his attention to Travis. "Will you keep an eye on him for a while longer?"

"Five bucks an hour." Travis smiled.

"Ha!" He thought quickly. "Collect it from Matt when we get home." He gave a peace sign before he shut the door and darted down the stairway.

The three men visited the restroom and grabbed themselves a drink before they collected a few supplies. Nick secured his slingshot and some M-80 firecrackers, whereas, Matt obtained flashlights.

Wrek slipped his sheath onto his belt as he walked into the laundry room, then he closed the door. He loaded the pipe and stashed his bag beneath a pile of towels before joining his brother-in-law and nephew on the bench.

The room was soon filled with smoke. They fixed their eyes onto the mirror, but nothing was stirring. Matt stood and stepped to the framed structure. "Mirror, mirror, on the wall . . ."

Wrek and Nick broke out in laughter.

Matt turned his upper build around and looked at them. "What?"

Still chuckling, they advanced toward him. "You have to talk nice to it." Wrek reached out and caressed the frame.

Matt pressed his fingers onto the glass. "Take us to the woman who needs our help." He felt a surge as an aura pulled them through.

It was almost dark as they stood on the gravel road next to the stolen car.

"Okay guys," Matt spoke quietly, "Let's smoke our last cigarettes and put your butts in your pockets. Don't leave any evidence or fingerprints anywhere." He paused as he lit his smoke. "And stay alert." They took off walking.

"We'll go in, grab the woman, and get out fast," Wrek added. "This guy is dangerous."

Nick choked when he heard his uncle's words.

Matt cast his attention to Nick's safety. "Maybe you should stand guard by the trees," he suggested, "Your mom would divorce me if anything happened to you."

"I want to help though," he insisted.

"You would be helping if you stood guard," Wrek confirmed. "If someone comes, you could light one of your firecrackers to warn us."

The men stood by a tall tree and inspected the area, taking note of a light that shone within a large window from the blue house.

The moon was aglow, just like the nearby city lights and they could hear the shrill, chirping sound of crickets.

The two rescuers left Nick at the tree and crept to the abode. They tiptoed window to window, peeking into the dark. "Are you sure they're in the house?"

"Unless they left," Wrek whispered, "But I did hear the man order her inside."

Nick played with his slingshot, sending small rocks across the dirt road. "Screw this," he told himself after a few minutes, then headed toward the house.

Matt and Wrek rounded the rear corner of the house and came upon the camper truck. They went to the window of the truck and peeked inside before walking to the hind part.

Matt opened the door of the camper and aimed his flashlight about. "I have an idea," he told Wrek as he stepped up to the base of the door. He advanced in and unhooked the fire extinguisher from its holder, then jumped to the ground. He carried the device to the back door of the house as Wrek followed.

"Wait!" Wrek warned, "I hear something."

They stood idle as they listened to the sound of footsteps coming closer.

"Nick?" Matt called out in a whisper.

Wrek quickly pulled the knife from his sheath as they concealed themselves to the exterior of the house and waited. A dark figure appeared.

"Matt? Uncle Wrek?"

Matt and Wrek exhaled their breath and stepped out. "I thought you were going to stand guard?"

"I wanted to be in on the action."

"Well you scared the crap out of us." Wrek lowered his knife.

They returned to the back door and tested the knob. It turned full course and Matt eased the door open. He observed a dark kitchen as he edged his way in. He could see a light shining from another room, perhaps the living room, he thought. As he tiptoed closer to the room, he heard the man talking on the telephone.

"Yea, I've got the bitch. I have her locked up."

Matt scanned the setup from where he stood against the edge of the wall. He looked at his comrades and pointed toward the hallway.

Without a sound, Wrek and Nick went to their knees and crawled toward the corridor. They came upon the first door and Wrek reached up and opened it. He peeked in and moved the flashlight about while Nick continued to the second door. As he pushed it open, it creaked.

"Oh shit," Matt lipped when he heard the noisy door from where he stood. He instantly unlocked the pin on the extinguisher and held the nozzle forward.

The abductor hung up the telephone. "Who's there?" he yelled.

Matt's heart was thumping with fear as he listened to the man stand and cock his pistol.

Wrek and Nick scampered into the bathroom.

The man hastened through the living room with His gun pointed.

Matt squeezed on the lever as he jumped out into the abductor's way. Foam sprayed onto his face.

The perpetrator roared in pain as he dropped to his knees and fired a few unsuccessful shots. With the man's vision impaired, Matt leaped behind and hit him atop of the head with the red container. When he saw that the man was unconscious, he dashed through the hallway. "Wrek, Nick! Hurry up and find that woman!"

They flipped on lights as they franticly searched every room. "I don't see her anywhere," they all spoke when they returned to the hallway.

"A secret room!" Matt suggested, "Look for trap doors."

They inspected the walls, looking for cracks or a concealed door opener. They checked bookcases, pulling books and videos to the floor.

Wrek hurried into the kitchen and studied the ceiling and then the floor. In the corner, he saw a hinged door that was padlocked shut. "Matt, Nick. Come here." He plunged to his knees and banged with his fist on the door. "Is anyone down there?" he yelled.

"Hello?" A soft voice came from within the tight closure of the door.

Wrek looked up at Matt. "She's in there. Find the key!"

Matt and Nick turned and ran into the living room. They quickly searched the tables for the device. Nothing. Matt sprang to the abductor, knelt, and stuck his hand into his pockets. "Aha!" he cheered as he removed and dangled the key for Nick to see.

"Let's hope it's the right one."

Matt arose and sped towards the kitchen while Nick followed. As he neared, he purposely dropped to his knees, sliding across the linoleum floor and bumped into Wrek. He then stuck the key into the rippled groove anticipating the click, and as fast as his hands would allow, he detached the lock from the hasp.

Wrek pulled the door upward and let it slam into the wall. They cast their eyes downward into the cellar and beheld a dark haired woman who was sitting on a step.

"We're here to help you. Come up." Matt and Wrek lowered their arms and offered their hands. "We won't hurt you."

The woman's face was bruised and puffy, she had been crying. "I'm scared," she said, "Paul will kill us."

"I'm scared too," Wrek spoke with urgency, "but we have to get out of here now."

She stood to her feet and crawled up the stairway. She reached up and took her rescuer's hands.

"My name is Wrek." They helped her to the floor and escorted her to the back door.

As they were exiting through the door, Paul came charging into the kitchen, firing unsteady shots toward them until the gun jammed.

"Run!" Nick who was nearest to the center of the room, yelled.

Wrek grabbed the woman's hand and fled to the outdoors where they ran toward the gravel road. Matt stopped at the exterior wall of the house, just a few feet from the door and looked for Nick to exit.

Paul who had blood visible upon his forehead, seized and wrapped his burly arm around Nick's neck, then pressed the pistol against his head. "What are you going to do now Beotch?" He was laughing and Nick was shaking. "A slut in exchange for a punk."

Nick's heart was pounding with fright. He felt as though he was going to vomit. "Please don't shoot me," he begged, "I'm only sixteen."

"Is that suppose to make me let you go?" He was breathing heavy. "Go get in the cellar!"

As he headed for the underground room, flashes came about and a green haze was apparent. In an instant, Nick was pulled through the mirror's force to home.

Matt saw through the kitchen window that his stepson was safe so he took off running towards Wrek and the woman who were waiting by the stolen car.

When Nick arrived and saw that he was alone in the laundry room, he fell to his knees. "Thank God," he cried in relief, then kissed the floor.

SIX

NISA WAUBAY

"My name is Nisa Waubay," the rescued woman told Wrek after she was done sobbing on his shoulder. "Thank you for saving me."

Wrek reached forward and grabbed a tissue from in between the front seats. "No more crying," he sympathized with her, "You're safe now."

Matt accelerated with great haste upon the gravel road, then sped out onto the blacktop. "He's not following us, is he?" He glanced into his rear view mirror.

Wrek turned his head and looked through the back window. "I think we're okay."

Matt lit a cigarette and cruised the speed limit. As he turned onto Central Avenue, he asked Nisa if she wanted to go to the hospital.

"No!" she quickly responded.

"Where do you want us to take you?" Wrek asked softly, "You need to put some ice on your face."

"My Aunt Penny's house. Paul doesn't know about her." She blew her nose. "She lives over on Sixth Street."

Through the darkness, Wrek tried to see if she was wearing a band on her ring finger.

"I don't know where Sixth Street is," Matt spoke, "so you'll have to give me directions." He puffed on his tobacco stick.

"Who are you guys?"

"We were walking by the alleyway when we heard you screaming," Wrek told her, "And then we saw that barbarian push you into his truck."

"And you followed me?"

"I rode on top of the camper," he quietly bragged, then spoke louder, "but yea, we followed."

"Wow. No one has ever wanted to help me before." She paused for a moment. "Can I have a cigarette?"

Wrek handed one to her and flicked his lighter as she held it between her lips. "Now let me ask you something." He held firm with his curiosity. "Why did Paul kidnap you?"

"I owe him money." She bowed her head. "I don't want to talk about it."

"Of course, I understand. I'm still a stranger to you."

Matt drove to where Nisa had instructed. Wrek walked her to the front door and while they stood on the lighted porch, he asked if he could call her.

She smiled in spite of her sore face.

He soon returned the expression before he reached his hand to her chin and gently touched it.

As they made small talk, she studied his features. His long brown curls reminded her of spiral noodles and his face was bathed with interest. "Why don't you stop by tomorrow? Maybe we could go have a drink."

His countenance grew sad. "I live too far away." He returned to the car with her phone number and sat in the passenger seat. He turned his head and watched this wonderful and hopefully, available woman enter into the house and close the door.

Matt sped off and drove two blocks. "We need to get rid of this car."

Wrek didn't say a word.

They were stopped at a red light when the air inside the vehicle became green and flashes came about.

After they were zapped through the mirror to home, they saw Nick lying on the bench, gazing up at the ceiling.

"I thought you were toast when Paul grabbed you," Matt asserted as he stepped to the bench.

"I thought so too," Nick replied as he sat up. "I had to check my drawers after that one," he bantered.

After discussing their adventure with a bowl of bud, Wrek got the boys ready for bed and they called it a night.

The next morning, Travis and Nathan awoke for school, but was running late because Nathan had pressed the snooze button a few times.

Matt entered into the kitchen and saw that Nathan was eating a breakfast burrito and Travis was munching on a piece of toast. "You two ready to go?"

"Almost."

"I'll go start up the truck."

The second bell was ringing when Matt dropped the tardy students at school. He then drove to Smelterville to his mom's house.

It was one o'clock when Matt returned home and saw Wrek napping on the couch. "Lazy bones," he told him.

Wrek popped an eye open. "I was awake when you left this morning." He coughed as he sat up. "Where were you?"

"My mom wanted me to bring some things down from her attic."

"Oh great! Did you bring home any more magical things?" he teased.

Matt chuckled. "No."

Wrek lit a cigarette and as he smoked, he let his mind wander. His thoughts were of Nisa; so petite and she had a helpless quality about her. The corner of his mouth arose as he pictured a future kiss.

Matt returned from the kitchen with a cola and sat on the couch close to his brother-in-law. He pulled a joint from his cigarette pack.

"I should call Nisa."

"And tell her you're in Idaho?" He lit the marijuana stick and inhaled.

"I'll tell her we caught a plane home."

The telephone rang. Matt arose, walked to the wall, and lifted the receiver. "Hello?"

"Matt. I don't feel good." Nathan moaned his words. "Will you come pick me up?"

"What's the matter?"

"My stomach hurts."

He thought for a moment. "Are you sure? You're mom warned me about your little scams."

"Yes, I'm sure," he fabricated. "I farted at least ten times in gym class."

Matt chuckled.

"My teacher even asked me if that was me blowing gas everywhere."

Some twenty minutes later and Matt arrived home with Nathan. "I want you in bed when you're done sitting on the toilet."

My pleasure, Nathan thought.

Wrek went into Dominique's office to use the telephone. "Hi Nisa. It's Wrek, your rescuer. How are you doing?" He fidgeted with the phone cord.

"I'm doing better now that you called," she replied.

"How's your face?"

"Still bruised in a few spots, but the swelling has gone down quite a bit."

"That's good." He paused. "Um . . . Are you married or have a boyfriend?"

"No. It's just me."

He cheered silently.

"I do have a daughter though, but she doesn't live with me."

"I bet she's as pretty as you," he remarked with cleverness.

"Prettier," she bragged, then there was silence. "I wish I could see you."

Evening had set in. Dinner was eaten and the boys were dusting and straightening the house, Matt came out of the laundry room carrying a basket. "Everyone's folding their own clothes." He dumped the dry clothes onto the couch.

The telephone rang. "I'll get it." Ian sprang to his stool and reached for the handset. "Hello?"

"Hi Baby Zebra."

"Mommy!"

Matt stepped to the excitement, aching to speak to his wife.

After talking to his mom, he handed the receiver to Matt. "Mommy's coming home next week," he whooped as he ran off to his bedroom.

Matt spoke to Dominique for several minutes, then to the back porch where Nick was tinkering with Travis' bicycle. "Your mom wants to go to Hawaii over Christmas break."

"Really? That's cool."

He lit a cigarette and looked up at the sky. As he puffed, he took note of the first star of the night. "Uh . . . I didn't tell your mom about the mirror, about our little adventure."

"Why not?" He set his wrench on the step and stood.

"I'll tell her in person, after she gets home."

"Yea, that would probably be best. She might not believe you." He slipped the front tire in between his legs and as he pressed his knees together, he pulled the handle bars back into place.

Matt took a few drags from his cigarette. "Your mom also said she's autographed about five hundred of her books already."

"That's a lot of books."

He watched his stepson tighten the bolt. "Not really. I've probably read about two thousand books in my lifetime."

Nick turned his eyes to Matt. "Someone's been in prison," he jested, "or you're a librarian."

He grinned. "The first one." He then dropped his cigarette onto the ground and stepped on it. "You want to go to the races this weekend?"

"I guess so." His brows drew together as he thought. "Why are you being nice to me?"

He ran a hand through his hair and sighed. "I don't hate you Nick." His mouth was dry as he spoke. "We need to call it truce, you think?"

"Maybe," he replied.

Ian fell asleep on the love seat. Matt and Nick came in from outside and joined Wrek on the couch who was smoking pot. Wrek passed the pipe to Matt and rested himself onto the backrest of the sofa. "I'm in love," he remarked.

"With Nisa?" Nick asked with an odd look upon his face. "You don't even know her."

"I know she'd look good on top of me," he grinned as he expressed shameless joy of self-satisfaction.

SEVEN

A VISIT

It was Friday morning when Matt arose from a lonely bed, stood in front of his bedroom window, and stretched. He peeked between the vertical blinds and observed a clear sky with the first dew of the season.

"Three days," he recalled of his wife's homecoming. He lit a cigarette and slipped into his clothes before heading out to see if Travis and Nathan were getting ready for school.

The two adolescents led the way as they were leaving through the door. Wrek entered the living room and spoke a quick good bye.

Matt turned to him. "I'll be home this afternoon." Then he closed the door.

Wrek looked at the clock. "Eight thirty-two. Hmm, I should go visit Nisa." He went to his room and collected his razor, his best casuals, his undergarments, and his shoes.

When he was done showering and dressing, he went into Ian's bedroom. "Wake up Sunshine. We're going bye bye."

"Where?" he asked with a yawn.

"It's a surprise."

Ian arose and dressed himself in his rugrats shirt and blue overalls. He walked out to where Wrek was waiting as he held a twisted strap over his shoulder. "I need help."

Wrek knelt and grabbed the strap. "Uh . . . did you go to the bathroom yet?"

"No."

"Go pee first, then I'll hook your overalls."

When Ian was dressed and ready, Wrek guided his young nephew into the laundry room.

"Why are we in here Uncle Wrek? Our bikes are outside."

"I know, but first I have to see if something works." He puffed on a joint as he took hold of Ian's hand and stood in front of the full length mirror. "Don't be scared if something funny happens," he told him, then looked into the glass and spoke, "Mirror, miror, please take me to Nisa. I need to see her."

Ian gazed up at his uncle with curiosity.

Wrek took another hit and exhaled the smoke before he reached forward with his hand and touched the glass. He felt a sudden onrush as the mirror began to activate. "Yes!" he exclaimed before they were pulled through.

Ian looked about the neighborhood with an open mouth. "Where are we?"

"We're in a large city where my girlfriend lives." He knocked the cherry off his joint as they headed down the block. They soon came upon Aunt Penny's house and when Wrek observed a rose bush that was growing close to the sidewalk, he quickly twisted a flowering stem until it broke off.

As he led the way to the anterior door, he took deep breaths to calm his nerves. He brought to mind, her black curls that reach just below her jawline and her eyes were seduce me green. Wrek stopped at the door and knocked before waiting for it to open. He knocked again.

The pearly white door opened as far as the security chain would allow. A familiar face peeked through. "Hi Wrek. What are you doing here?" she asked with a smile.

"I came to see you." He extended the red rose into her view and returned her friendly expression.

Her heart fluttering with curiosity, Nisa closed the door, unlatched the chain, and repoened the door. She took hold of the flower and smelled it. "Did you pick this from our bush?" She continued to smile as she minded his blue eyes.

"You caught me."

"Come on in." She backed up. "Who's your little friend?"

"This is my nephew, Ian."

"Hi Ian," she welcomed.

He returned the greeting in a soft voice.

"I'm babysitting for my sister while she's on tour."

Nisa gave him an odd look. "On tour? Is she famous or something?"

"Not really famous. She wrote a novel."

"Oh wow! That's awesome." She closed the door and locked it. "So did she get rich from her book?"

"Uhh . . . she's well off."

"Come sit down. I was just sipping on some coffee. You want some?"

"Sure." He and Ian sat on the couch while Nisa fetched him a cup from the kitchen.

She returned and set the cup of hot liquid on the coffee table upon a coaster.

"Thank you," Wrek spoke.

"I have some ice cream, chocolate, if your nephew wants some."

Wrek cast his eyes to Ian who was shaking his head no.

Nisa sat in her chair and picked up the remote. "Do you want to watch cartoons Ian?" She clicked the channel to a children's station. While he watched TV, Wrek and Nisa engaged in conversation.

"You smoke pot?" Wrek asked her.

"Sometimes. I prefer to drink beer." She took a cigarette out from her pack and lit it. "Why? Do you have some?"

He smiled and nodded his head.

"Okay, I'll take a few tokes."

"What about your Aunt Penny, is she going to come in here and catch us?"

"No, she left for work already."

He drew his bag and pipe out from his pants pocket. "So have you heard from Paul or seen him?"

"No. I haven't been out of this house. I'm still too afraid to walk to the corner market by myself."

"Damn! You should get yourself a gun," he suggested as he passed her the pipe.

"I don't like guns."

"Maybe not, but it would stop him from hurting you again."

She took a toke and coughed. "I could think about it."

He sipped from his coffee. "You have a picture of your daughter?"

"Yes I do." She stood, walked to the bookshelf, and embraced a framed photo. "You have any kids?" she asked as she turned herself to face him.

"No, never had the pleasure."

She discharged an odd look his way. "You never had sex before?"

"No," he chuckled. His eyes held a hint of embarrassment. "I meant that I've never been married or had a serious girlfriend."

"Why not?" she spoke with interest as she looked upon his face, absorbing in his pointy nose and limited facial hair. "You seem like a nice enough guy." She handed him the picture.

"I don't know." He looked at the photo. "Maybe I haven't met the right woman." He lifted and set his range of vision to hers. "Until now."

Nisa was momentarily speechless to his comment.

"You want to be my girlfriend?"

Her face grew blush as she smiled.

Wrek scooted to the edge of the couch and leaned in toward her. "Don't be scared," he whispered, "I can make you feel good and happy."

She twiddled her thumbs. "And how could you do that?" she asked in a soft voice.

"I could start by giving you a massage." He flashed his eyebrows quickly.

Nisa glanced at Ian who was still attentive to the TV program.

"He'll be okay," Wrek assured.

"But I just met you a few days ago." She tried to fight the urge.

"You deserve a rub," he coaxed, "That's all I'll do, unless you say othewise."

She nodded.

Wrek stood and offered her a hand. They took their drinks and smokes into the small bedroom that was lighted and arranged with a day bed in the midst of many tall and bushy plants.

"This is an awesome room." He beheld the green jungle pose and the mirror on the closet doors which made the area feel larger. He sat beside Nisa on the converter and soon he drove his hand to her back.

"Do you want me to take off my shirt and lay down?"

He was excited from her question, but didn't show it. "Yea."

Nisa grabbed the hem of her shirt and with both hands, she slowly pulled up.

Wrek's anticipation grew. His eyes widened. "Oh my God," he stammered when he saw her balloon shaped breasts bounce from the lifting of her shirt. "They're beautiful!" he mumbled as he gawked at her hard nipples.

She scooted to the center of the bed and rolled to her stomach.

He adjusted his sitting position and touched his hands onto her soft tawny skin. He felt his own sexual organ begin to swell.

"Oh . . . That feels so good. You were right," she moaned as he squeeze rubbed her shoulders.

"Do you know what a minikin is?" he asked.

"No."

"It's a small delicate creature." He paused. "Like you."

"That's sweet," she remarked, "But a creature? Aren't animals just the creatures?"

"Sure, but we're all God's creations." He moved his hands across her scapula and down her sides for a feel of her bosom.

He rubbed another few minutes before he asked for a kiss.

She rolled to her backside, exposing again, her units.

Wrek leaned downward and while he pressed his lips to hers, he transported his hand onto her left bust and applied gentle pulls.

She moaned.

He kissed her cheek before working his kisses to her points. He lifted his head and as he watched his hand caress her, he observed the surrounding air turning green. Damn it, he thought. "I have to go!" he abruptly announced as he stood to his feet.

"Why?" The pleasure left her face.

He grabbed his cigarettes and darted out of the room. "I'll call you." He raced into the living room, took hold of Ian's hand, and hurried out of the house. After he closed the door, they disappeared in through the structure of the atmosphere and came out into the laundry room of Dominique's house.

"I wasn't done watching that show Uncle Wrek!" Ian scolded.

"I wasn't done either," Wrek agreed as he let go of his nephew's hand and darted to the bathroom where he closed and locked the door. He stepped into the tub and unzipped his jeans, then commenced to care for his erection.

The town clock sounded its noon bell when Matt pulled into the driveway and turned off the engine. After he stepped out and closed the truck door, he observed Wrek pedaling up the sidewalk towards him. "You took Ian to school, huh?"

"That, and I stopped at the store for munchies." He withdrew himself from the bicycle and pushed it as far as the carport. "Done helping your mom?"

"Yea, the attic is cleared out."

Wrek was sensing Matt's merry mood as they entered into the house. They saw Nick yawning while he stepped slowly down the staircase.

"He's awake!"

Nick who was dressed with his boxers sticking out from his jeans, led the way to the kitchen where he and Matt nabbed themselves a drink. Wrek dumped his bag of groceries onto the counter top.

"What kind of munchies did you get?" Matt asked as he looked over his shoulder.

"Donuts, chips, chocolate bars, umm . . . strawberry milk."

"Dude! You're going to rot out your teeth even faster."

All was quiet for a number of moments as they stood around drinking their pops. Wrek turned and leaned his tail end against the counter ledge. "I did something," he spoke in a deep voice as he bowed his head. "I want to come clean."

Nick grinned. "Ohh . . ." he expressed in a childish tone, "He wants to confess."

Wrek looked up at Nick and returned the smile. "I went and visited Nisa this morning."

"The mirror let you?" Matt waited with anticipation for an answer.

"Yea, I just asked it to take me to Nisa and then I touched . . ."

"Wait a minute," he interupted, "Where was Ian?"

"Yea," Wrek hesitated, "He went with me."

Nick stepped in closer to his uncle. "So he knows About the mirror?"

"You can't take him through the mirror anymore," Matt reproved, "he will tell people."

"I won't do it again." He gave his word. "But I want to tell you that I almost got laid."

"Almost?" They were curious.

"I was rubbing and sucking on her beautiful breastesses and then that stupid mirror activated and brought us back home."

"Ha ha!" Nick teased.

He explained how he had left abruptly. "It's as if that mirror is protecting her." He reached into his shirt pocket and took hold of his pack of cigarettes. "It wouldn't even let me screw her."

Matt and Nick fixed their attention upon his next words.

"It showed us her kidnapping and it took us back to rescue her."

"And why?" Matt wondered as he thought.

Wrek lit his stick and puffed. "We may not know why the mirror is protective of Nisa, but I do know I'll keep trying to bone her."

EIGHT

RUNAWAY

THE SUN BROUGHT Monday morning in with a warm and cheery breeze. It was the start of week three for the boys as they attended school. Wrek walked uptown to apply for a job while Matt and Nick drove to the city, to the airport.

"It'll be nice to have your mom home again," Matt remarked as he steered his truck onto Terminal Drive.

Wrek's interview went grand. He accepted the position of second cook and walked out of the restaurant with a smile. He strolled home, thinking of Nisa and how he'd like to see her again.

Matt and Nick were standing by Gate Five where they waited for the plane to roll into the boarding area and off-load the passengers. Matt's heart was pounding with excitement as he watched Dominique walk through the bridge toward him. She stepped closer and closer.

"You look good," Matt whispered his charm into her ear as he wrapped his muscular arms about her tiny body.

"I hate flying. I was so scared."

Matt brought up his hand and lifted her face so when her lonely eyes met to his, he leaned down and kissed her.

"Mmm," she moaned, "I missed your lips." When she was done greeting Matt, she turned and gave her son a hug. "I'm so glad to be home, I missed my family."

"I think Ian missed you the most," Nick recounted. "He was sad one night and cried."

"Ohh . . . I feel awful for leaving." She enfolded her hand into Matt's. "Next time I'll have to take him with me." They took off walking toward the baggage claim.

Wrek entered into his sister's empty house and after closing the front door, he glanced at the clock. "Twelve-twenty one, I still have a couple of hours," he spoke to himself as he walked to the bathroom and checked his hair and combed his mustache. He then stepped into the laundry room and sat on the stoner's bench where he toked on his pipe and gazed at the looking glass.

Soon the air was filled with smoke. Wrek slipped his pipe into his pocket and stood before the framed glass. "Mirror, please take me to Nisa." He extended his arm and touched the mirror. He rubbed the edging as he spoke softly of his minikin, but he felt no surge. He noted the air wasn't turning color, nor were there any flashes. "Don't be mad at me, I like Nisa." He continued to pet it. "I wouldn't do anything to hurt her." For a brief time, he begged the mysterious mirror to exert its force and draw him through, but he soon returned to the bench with disappointment. "Stupid mirror," he mumbled.

The school bus stopped in front of Dominique's estate and let Ian off. He ran across the yard and threw the anterior door open. "Mommy?" he called out.

Wrek stepped into the living room. "She's not home yet."

He plopped himself onto the couch and began to cry.

"She'll be home any minute," he comforted his nephew as he knelt beside the sofa. "Why don't you go get your welcome home sign and all your pictures you drew for her."

When Ian arose from the sofa, the telephone rang. Wrek took an upright position and walked to the wall where he picked up the receiver. A soft voice transmitted through the wires. "Nisa?" he was stunned. "Hi . . . I was going to call you."

"I was wondering." She was sitting on her chair and with her finger, she wound her hair.

"Yea, I've been busy," he replied.

"You ran out on me."

"I know I did Babe, I'm sorry about that."

"Why did you leave?"

"Uh, I didn't want to take advantage of you," he quickly bid.

There was a pause. "When will I see you?" she asked.

Without thinking, he spoke, "In a few days."

Travis and Nathan rushed through the door and threw their backpacks onto the floor. "Mom?"

Wrek observed his nephews. "I have to go," he told his girl. "My sister's kids are all home now and it's getting noisy."

"Call me later," she urged.

"I will Babe." He ended the connection and joined in on the chaos.

Matt parked in the driveway and before he, Nick, and Dominique could exit the truck, the anxious gang was hovering around the vehicle. Ian jumped into his mother's arms and held on tight.

"I take it you missed me." She embraced her baby. "Next time, Mommy's taking you with me." She kissed him repeatedly before putting him down and turning her attention to Travis and Nathan.

"I'm off grounded now," Nathan reminded his mom.

Wrek and Nick grabbed Dominique's suitcases from the bed of the truck and carried them into the house. Matt watched from behind as his wife walked upon the sidewalk toward the house. "Damn!" he spoke under his breath. He was wanting to get her alone.

The family gathered into the living room and exchanged opinions and stories for the next hour.

Nathan requested to leave. "Can I go to Sandy's house?"

"Be home at eight thirty," Matt acknowledged as he took note of Dominique yawning and stretching. "It looks like you need to go rest," he told her with a smile.

"Rest my ass!" Wrek blurted, "You're going to . . ." He held his tongue.

"They're going to kiss," Ian replied, "Just like Uncle Wrek and Nisa."

Dominique looked at her brother, questioning him with a tacit expression.

"She's my girlfriend."

"Dominique," Matt spoke as he leaned her way. "I'll explain later where he met her."

Everyone was quiet. "Well, I guess," Dominique said as she stood, "I'm going to go take a bubble bath and try to scam a backrub." She peered at Matt.

"I don't do backrubs," he grumbled.

She gave him a dirty look. "Thanks a lot."

He changed his mind. "Okay." He then followed her to the master bedroom. She entered and locked the door. As she strolled to the bathtub, she stripped.

The next morning, Dominique awoke to Matt's lustful hands upon her breasts. She opened her eyes and smiled at him.

"We still have thirteen days to make up for," he whispered to her. He lifted her nightgown over her head and let her naked body be on display for his pleasures.

After a late morning, Matt and Dominique stepped into the kitchen where Wrek was assisting Ian with his hot chocolate. "Mmm, I love the smell of your fresh, brewed coffee," she spoke to her brother as she joined them at the counter. "Good morning Baby Zebra." She kissed him atop of his head, then grabbed herself a regular morning soda.

"Mommy, I'm going to play cop today."

"That's fine. Just don't arrest ME."

Matt approached his wife. "What are you going to do today?" he asked as he lit a cigarette.

"I have to go grocery shopping," she replied as she watched Ian stir his drink.

"Will you buy me some pudding?" the boy petitioned.

She nodded.

Wrek dawdled as he stepped to his sister and spoke. "Dominique? Can I ask a big favor of you?" He took a puff from his tobacco stick. "And remember, I did just watch your kids for two weeks."

"What is it?"

"An airline ticket. Round trip to Phoenix for two days."

She carried a puzzled expression upon her face.

Matt stepped in. "Let's go sit on the stoner's bench and talk."

The following week went by swiftly for Dominique and her clan. Wrek returned happy from visiting Nisa, anxious to start his new job while Dominique was able to catch up on housework and errands. Everyday, she gave thought to the incredible tale, as told by her husband and brother, of them being forced through a physical piece of furniture and saving a woman's life.

It was late Friday afternoon when Matt left in his truck to go fishing. Nick and Nathan joined in on the adventure and the three fellows headed for the North Fork. Wrek had to work.

Travis was sitting with Dominique at the kitchen table discussing his life when they heard the sound of glass breaking. They jumped up and hurried out to the backyard. "Ian?"

"He's under the trampoline," Travis spoke of his little brother.

She scanned the area for broken glass as she walked to the bouncing apparatus. She knelt. "Are you hurt?" She could see the fear in his face.

"No."

"Come here." She stretched her arm forward to help him get out. "Show me what got broken." She quickly inspected his hands.

They walked to the garage where she observed a hole in the window and pieces of glass on the ground.

"You were throwing rocks, weren't you?" She was stern with her question.

"It was just a PLAY rock," he pleaded as he began to cry.

"You go to your bedroom!" she ordered, "You're in big trouble."

He ran across the lawn toward the house and pushed on the partially open back door.

"Were you a bad boy?" Travis jested quietly.

"Shut up!" Ian bellowed, "You're a narc!"

"Whoa!" Travis expressed with a half grin, "Don't be mad at me."

Ian stopped at the living room entrance, turned, and looked at his brother. "I'm having a bad day, okay?" He took off running to his bedroom.

After Dominique swept away the pieces of broken glass, she went into the house and lit a cigarette. She sat at the table and considered Ian's punishment.

Twenty minutes passed by when Dominique decided to go talk to her son. She approached his bedroom and after giving a quick knock, she opened the door. She moved her eyes around the room, then stepped in. "Ian?" She knelt and viewed underneath his bed before checking the closet and his large toy box. "Maybe he's in the bathroom," she suggested to herself.

She searched the entire upper section of the house before returning to the main floor. Travis was in the kitchen. "Ian's not in his room. Have you seen him?"

"No," he replied with concern.

"You go check outside while I search the rest of the house." She hurried to the main floor restroom while Travis rushed out to the yards.

Dominique walked into the laundry room and switched on the light. She glanced behind the door before going to the rear of the looking glass for a peek. When she stepped to the face of the mirror, she cast her eyes to the floor and saw

Ian's stuffed tiger sitting against the washer. She knelt and lifted Duhe up to her chest. As she held the soft toy, she gave thought to Matt's tall tale. She looked into the glass surface. "Could it be possible?"

Ian, a defiant runaway, walked alone upon a sidewalk in the city of Phoenix. He was a little worried as he strolled by a few houses, hoping to find Uncle Wrek's girlfriend. He came upon a blue house, a yellow house, and a white house before coming to another yellow house that looked familiar. He took note of the rose bush located by the sidewalk where he remembered his uncle had picked a flower.

He stepped to the front door and reached up to press the doorbell. As he waited for the door to open, he picked his nose and wiped a booger on the door frame.

The milky colored door opened. He looked up and saw a fat woman who had orange hair and wore glasses.

"Well hello little guy," she greeted.

The adolescent portrayed nervousness within his brown eyes. "Is Nisa here?" his voice quivered. It all seemed so right the moment he went through the mirror, but now he was wanting his mom.

Aunt Penny observed his innocence. She smiled and noted his tiny spiked nose and long eyelashes. "She is. Come in." She stepped back and let him enter. "Have a seat, I'll go get her."

After he walked in, he took in the scent of bread as it baked. He thought it smelled like bananas.

Penny closed the door and went towards the hallway where she disappeared into a room.

Ian was sitting on the sofa when Nisa appeared into the living room. "Oh wow," she breathed with surprise. "What are you doing here?" She sat down beside her odd guest.

"I got into trouble," he replied with a hint of shyness.

"Uh . . ." She didn't quite know what to say. "Where is your Uncle Wrek or mom?"

"My mom is at home."

"How did you get here?" She thought more about the situation and decided to fish for information. "Do you live close to my house?"

"The mirror."

"The mirror?" she repeated. "I don't know of any mirror."

"You talk to it and it sucks you in," he tried to explain.

Dominique darted to the exit of the laundry room and yelled for Travis.

He rushed to the call. "What is it?"

"Come here," she motioned. "I think Ian went through the mirror."

"Huh?"

"Stand beside me." She was contemplating on what to say when the telephone rang. She turned her eyes toward Travis. "Let me answer that real quick."

As Nisa waited for Dominique to arrive, she offered the tad a snack and a drink, then escorted him out to the back porch where they sat on a bench swing. She made small talk. "When is your birthday?"

"Febuary eighth."

"Cool. Mine is February twentieth. What year?"

He looked at her with confusion. "Every year," he answered.

NINE

NISA'S PLAN

MATT AND HIS two stepsons arrived home from fishing. As they were removing the cooler from the bed of the truck, Dominique turned on the porch light and stepped outside. She walked to her husband for conversation. "I need to talk to you."

Nick observed her presence and opened the lid. "Look at my catch," he bragged.

She leaned in for a peek. "Wow!"

"Sixteen inches," he replied as he continued to explain how he caught it. He returned the lid to the rim and carried the cooler to the rear of the house.

Matt and Dominique cast their eyes upon each other. "I believe you," she told him.

"About what?"

"About your tall tale."

He thought for a moment. "Why do you believe me now?"

She told him of Ian's adventure and how she had to go through the mirror to bring him home.

Inside the house, Dominique walked to the main floor bathroom and after going in, she picked up a brush and swept her hair as she stood in front of the sink. She gave heavy thought to and then decided she would box up that mahogany troublemaker. "I'm not going to chance my son's whereabouts again." She layed the bristly device down and turned off the light before going to the closet in her office where she collected a roll of bubble wrap and tape.

Soon she was in the laundry room, wrapping the legs of the mirror. When she brought the roll around the base of the glass, she saw a few green specks blowing out into the air as though the mirror was resisting. She feared being pulled through to a strange place so she turned the reflective surface away from her.

She continued to swathe the mirror. "Ouch!" She looked down at her finger, for she had been pricked by a splinter.

Ian appeared by the door and yawned. "Mommy. Are you going to put me to bed?"

She was made aware of the time as she turned. "Of course. It's that late already?"

"I think so." The five year old led the way to his bedroom. He was already dressed in his pajamas so he just climbed into bed. Dominique pulled the blankets away and then back across him.

"I need to talk to you about something."

She sat at the end of his car shaped bed and gave her attention to him.

"I wanna talk about Christmas." His eyes gleamed.

She smiled because she knew where this conversation was leading.

"I want a ladder!"

"A ladder? Why would you want a ladder?"

"So me and Nick can have a ladder match with Travis and Nathan."

She tried to picture his idea of the ladder positioned along side the trampoline with the play belt looped over the top step.

"Can I have one?" Eagerness emitted from his face.

"We'll see." She stood and stepped to him.

"I'm sorry for running away Mommy," he spoke as he snuggled into his pillow.

She lifted and reset Duhe beside him. "I understand, I know you didn't mean to." She kissed him good night. As she left the room, she focused in on her throbbing finger and went straightway to the bathroom where she extracted the wooden piece.

When she returned to the laundry room, Matt and Wrek were standing at the doorway. "What are you doing?" It was asked after they saw the bubble wrapped mirror.

"This thing has to go!" she demanded. "Will you carry it out of here?"

"Take it where?" Wrek began to panic. "That's my access to Nisa." He stepped to his sister.

Dominique sighed. "Put it in the garage then." She left the room. "And keep it wrapped."

Nisa eyed the clock, making sure she had enough time to cut and paste before Aunt Penny arrived home from work. Her thoughts were of Wrek and his sister's money.

She poured herself a glass of wine and pulled the gauzy yellow curtain across the window. She sat at the kitchen table and placed some art supplies around a piece of paper. She unfolded and slipped a pair of latex gloves onto her hands before skimming through a magazine. She scissored a few large letters and arranged them to form her first word.

It was nearing four o'clock when Nisa picked up and discarded the paper scraps. She addressed the envelope, then folded the dried letter and slipped it into the white receptacle. "Nisa, you're a bright girl," she told herself as she uplifted and kissed her plan.

The slender woman stamped the mailer and walked to the sink where she rinsed her glass. She lit herself a cigarette and left the kitchen. She went outside to the hot weather where she strolled the sidewalk to the corner and slipped her letter into the blue mailbox. She looked up the street and saw the postal vehicle. "Just in time."

Nick was waxing his new car, trying to get it done before the rain set in. He had his Dodge Charger parked in the driveway ready to be wheeled in through the open garage door.

Matt stood within the house looking out the bay window remembering his and Dominique's argument. As he watched Nick, he gritted his teeth. He thought it wasn't right that he had that car.

A grizzled truck neared and parked next to the curb. Matt turned his attention to the driver who was approaching the sidewalk. He took note of the man's posture, then his hair and facial features. "Oh cool." He shifted and headed toward the door.

Dominique stepped into the room with a handful of chicken bites. "Bye," she told him as she leaned up against the entry support and popped a chunk of meat into her mouth.

"I'll just be outside." He closed the door.

She went to the window. She set her eyes upon Matt who was walking the sidewalk toward Nick and a stranger. "Hmm?" she questioned as she admired the stranger's muscular build.

"Dash Bradly!" Matt greeted. "It's good to see you."

"Yea, you too. I wanted to get over here earlier, but you know how that goes."

Matt pulled a cigarette from his pack. "You still staying with your sister in Smelterville?"

"Sort of. I'm living in a small trailer in her backyard."

Matt nodded and took a drag before turning toward Nick. "This is my wife's oldest boy."

The trio talked for a few minutes, then Matt invited his ex-cellmate to come into the house to meet Dominique.

"The writer?" Dash corroborated.

They stepped to the porch and entered through the face door. They went into the living room and approached Dominique. She was in her chair with the remote control, clicking through the different channels.

"Dominique. This is my buddy Dash."

She pressed the mute button and acknowledged his presence. "Hello."

Dash didn't let it show, but he was awed by her appearance as he studied her intently.

The telephone rang. Travis and Nathan who were both expecting calls, fought to answer it.

"That's enough of that shit!" Wrek spoke as he came up behind them and grabbed the receiver. The boys waited in anticipation as their uncle talked. He looked at his nephews and covered the mouthpiece. "It's for me."

"Oh . . . ," they moaned as they walked away.

Wrek turned aside. "What's the matter?" he asked his caller.

"I need to see you," Nisa who proclaimed to be upset, said. "Can you come through the mirror?"

"I don't know," he replied, "Last time I tried, it wouldn't let me."

A half hour later, Wrek who was wearing flashy garments and smelled of cologne, stepped into the kitchen where Travis was making himself a sandwich. "Where's your mom?" he asked.

"She went to the store."

He looked closer at what Travis was cutting. "What are you doing?" He expressed an odd look.

"I'm taking the seeds out of this tomato."

"Why?"

Travis smiled. "Cuz I don't like the seeds."

"You're weird!" He stepped away. "Tell your mom . . ., never mind. I'll see you later." He left the kitchen.

Without anyone seeing him, Wrek exited the house and went into the garage where the unusual mirror occupied the far corner. He moved the large looking glass away from the two conjoined walls and as he peeled the bubble wrap, the mirror purred. "What?" he questioned under his breath, then turned the reflector around. He lifted his arm and as he petted the frame, he talked. "Nice mirror. Please take me to Nisa." He soon saw a green vapor come forth and arise from the glass. He was taken through.

Nisa was on the telephone with her friend of two years. She puffed on her cigarette as she sat in the recliner with her legs draped off the arm. "Call me back and let me know," she stressed.

"It'll be about ten, fifteen minutes."

"That's okay, I'll be here." She hung up the phone and gave strict thought to her plan.

"Sweet!" Wrek uttered after he landed on his feet onto a sidewalk. He looked around and began to head toward the direction of Sixth Street. He walked around the block and came upon Aunt Penny's house. He stopped, took his small knife out of his pocket, and cut the stem of a rose from the bush. He proceeded with excitement to the door and then he knocked.

Nisa opened the door. "Wrek," she welcomed, "You're here, and you picked another flower."

He handed it to her.

"My aunt is going to get mad at you." Her eyes twinkled.

"Mad, shmad." He bit his lower lip. "The mirror gave me no problem. I think it likes me now."

She leaned in and gave him a kiss. "What do you mean it likes you now?"

"I freed it from the bubble wrap."

"Huh?"

"Long story, my Minikin." He pulled a cigarette from his pack.

"I do have the time to listen."

"But you needed to talk to me?" He lit the tobacco stick.

"Yes, I did," she replied, "I've been getting crank phone calls." She walked to the coffee table and picked up an envelope. "I also received this in the mail today."

Wrek went to her and took the document. "Who do you think's been crank calling?"

She shrugged her shoulders. "I don't know."

"What do they say?"

"Nothing."

He examined the address and observed the markings. "It was postmarked yesterday. here in Phoenix." He looked at her. "Maybe it's Paul."

The telephone rang. Nisa perched herself onto the sofa and lifted the receiver. "Hello?"

"Hey Nisa, it's me. The price for the . . ."

"Hello?" Nisa spoke again, but with more vexation in her voice.

Her friend began to repeat her words.

"Don't call and not talk." She slammed the handset down onto the base and turned her eyes upon Wrek who was exhibiting a look of concern. "Another crank call," she fabricated.

Wrek drew the paper from the envelope and read the letter pasted message. "FIFTY THOUSAND OR YOU WILL BE SORRY."

As she bowed her head, she put her hands over her face and produced tears. "I don't understand that message Wrek," she sobbed. "I don't have any money."

He sat and put his arm onto her dorsal area. "Have you talked to anyone else about this?"

"No."

He thought for a moment, then looked at her. "You told me you owed Paul some money. Why?"

She reached to the coffee table, nabbed a tissue, and after blowing her nose, she spoke. "He bailed me out of a sticky situation one time."

"Jail?"

She nodded. "That and other things."

"I'm listening if you want to tell me." He dabbed his cigarette into the ashtray.

"I got myself into trouble." She paused as she choked on her words. "Robbery. They took my daughter." She turned on the tears again.

With his arm fixed upon her back, he held her closer to indicate sympathy. "Do you think he sent the letter?"

"Perhaps." She was nervous as she tried to keep the blame on Paul. "But I don't want to call him to try and verify it."

"No, he's kind of dangerous."

"I'm scared Wrck." They nestled backwards into the couch.

He felt compelled to offer his assistance. "What can I do to help?"

She sat forward. "Do you know where to get fifty grand?"

TEN

NATHAN'S IDEA

Dominique stepped inside the living room from the front porch carrying Saturday's mail. As she stood in her office, she dropped the slew of envelopes atop of her desk and rummaged through them. She selected the letter that brought a smile to her face; the letter from her agent. She opened the folded paper, pulled the document out, and read: "Two hundred thousand and . . ." Her eyes widened. "Yes!" She set the check down and after she touched her palms together in front of her, she quickly rubbed them simultaneously, causing friction.

Matt entered into the room and observed his wife's blissfulness. "Did your check come today?"

She turned and looked at him. "Yes," she nodded, then approached him with the bank note. "Look at it!"

Nathan walked past his mom's office door, then returned and stopped. "Mom, I'm bored."

"Did you sweep the garage yet?" Matt brought to mind.

"No."

"It'll take you ten minutes, then I can find more work for you."

Nathan was swift to respond. "I'll sweep the garage and find something to do."

Matt left the room with his stepson. "Don't forget," he whispered, "Your mom's surprise party tonight at six."

"I won't." He walked within the kitchen and exited through the rear door where his legs led him to the garage.

Travis came trotting across the crisp sallow lawn and joined his brother. "Where are you going?" he asked.

"In here." He pointed. "I have to sweep."

Travis followed him inside.

Nathan pushed the button that hoisted the large automatic door. After the sunlight shone in, he observed his mother's mirror, unwrapped and standing alone in the corner. He questioned Travis about it.

He shrugged his shoulders.

Nathan was just about done with his sweeping when Nick pulled in and parked his car along side the building. He shut down the engine and secured his vehicle before walking into the garage. "Hey, it's Pueblo and his brother."

With the broom, Nathan flung a pile of dirt toward him.

Nick jumped out of the way and chuckled.

Before long, Nathan was pacing about the mirror, looking at it, then casting his eyes toward his brothers. He did this a few times, then asked Nick how it worked.

"Why?"

"It takes you places, right?"

Nick nodded.

"Well, let's go see our cousins, Chris and Sean."

"It's only taken us to Arizona."

"We could try Kentucky?" Travis suggested as he stepped into the conversation.

"Uh . . ." Nick thought. "Yea, but the only way to activate the miror is to smoke pot and talk to it."

"What are we waiting for?" Nathan encouraged, "I'll go sneak a bud from Uncle Wrek."

"Grab his pipe too!"

Nick closed the automatic garage door and smoked on a cigarette while Travis stood as lookout at the side door.

Dominique poured some chocolate milk into a small plastic cup and carried it with her to Ian's bedroom. She sat next to her son on the bed and dispensed a dose of liquid pain reliever into his mouth, then watched him drink the brown milk.

He laid back down and cuddled with Duhe, his sleeping time buddy.

"My poor baby," she whispered as she touched her palm to his forehead.

Wrek entered the room. "Is he still warm?"

"Oh-yea. Hundred and one. The doctor said he wouldn't feel better until tomorrow."

Ian closed his eyes.

Wrek stepped closer and spoke quietly, "I need to talk to you."

"Wait until later, okay?" She cast her eyes upon him.

"Yea, sure," he replied.

"Is it the kind of talk that we do in my office or on the stoner's bench?"

"Mmm, the bench." He wanted her to be high when he asked for the money.

Nathan returned to the garage.

Travis closed and locked the door before turning on the light.

Nathan pulled the items from his pocket and handed them to Nick. "I sure hope we don't get caught. Mom will ground us for life."

"Or until we're eighteen," Travis simplified.

"Speak for yourselves. She'll take my car away," Nick speculated as he put the bud into the pipe's bowl.

The three adventure seekers stood in front of the mirror. Nick toked first, then handed the pipe and lighter to his fourteen year old brother who had never smoked a day in his life. They watched as Travis inhaled and coughed. Next, it was the pre-teen, who also inhaled and choked on the smoke.

After a few puffs, Nick reached out and stroked the frame of the reflector. "Mirror, mirror. Please take us to Oak Grove, Kentucky." He inhaled and blew the smoke onto the glass. It became green. "It's going to work!" He glanced at his siblings, then he was engulfed.

Their eyes widened and their mouths dropped. They looked at each other. "Awesome!" Travis spoke, then he was pulled through.

Nathan brushed himself up against the speculum. Green sparks shot out from the glass and he was swallowed up.

When he came into existence in his new destination, he was standing beside Travis. He cast his eyes about and saw, not too far away, a fueling station with a great number of freight trucks. He turned and observed the corn field behind them. "Where's Nick?"

"I don't know," Travis replied with worry.

Nathan encircled his hands around his mouth and called out for his brother. He heard no reply.

"We should walk to that gas station. Maybe he's there." They took off walking across the parking lot.

Nick was waiting on Sixth Street for Travis and Nathan to pop through. He knew he wasn't in Kentucky because he recognized the area. He inserted a pinch of chew between his lower lip and gum and as he began to slowly walk the sidewalk, he spied the area for the two truants. When he neared the end of the block, he observed a familiar truck turning onto his street. As the vehicle advanced, he glanced at the driver who in return, looked at him. "Oh shit," he breathed when he recognized the man to be Paul.

"Hey!" Paul yelled and threw on the brakes.

Nick took off running in the opposite direction.

Travis and Nathan asked the cashier for directions to Lillian Drive.

"Half a mile down the road," she told them.

They trekked on the edge of the narrow road, passing a dollar store, a police station, then a small cemetery.

"I wonder where Nick was taken to?"

"Maybe he's already at Chris and Sean's." Nathan suggested.

With his adrenaline pumping, the muscular teenager darted around the corner. Taking his turn too wide, Nick bumped his knee onto a fire hydrant. "Ah . . . son of a bitch!" he cried out as he dropped to the sidewalk. He grabbed his injury and as he sat up, he glanced back to see the truck reversing out from Sixth Street. He quickly stood. He heard the grinding of the gears as Paul shifted into first. Nick gritted his teeth and limped as he continued to flee. He turned into the alley and in spite of his excruciating pain, he sprinted.

Just as the truck came roaring behind him, Nick took a quick left, exiting through an open gate. He sped beyond the measure of the grass, dashed around the house and left the yard. He crossed Fifth Street and when he was midway through a lot, he heard the truck coming around the block.

Nick scanned the nearby yard as he persevered toward it. He saw a small plastic pool that was leaned against the garage, so he seized the edge and as he laid on the dry grass, he slipped the unfilled water device atop of him. He was dripping sweat and trying to catch his breath while he listened to the sound of Paul's truck drive by and then disappear.

Nathan and Travis came to Lillian Drive. They turned the corner and walked pass a small island in the street, then arrived at their cousin's house. They viewed their property. There were no vehicles parked in the driveway and a newspaper hung from the front door knob.

"They're not even home," Travis said after knocking on the door.

"I don't see Nick anywhere either."

The two thrill seekers headed to the back yard where they peeked through a window. "I see a black dog," Nathan reported.

"This sux. We came here for nothing," Travis spoke as be backed away from the glass. "Come on. Aunt Rachel and Uncle Randy probably took them on a road trip. They're always doing that, you know."

Nathan thought for a moment. "No. They wouldn't leave the dog."

They sat down on a wooden bench and scoped out the yard. "I'm thirsty."

Nick was in a hunched position, lying on the cement floor of the garage when Nathan and Travis returned home, via the mirror.

"Cool, everyone's home safely," Travis commented as he stepped and looked at Nick. "Where were you?"

"Phoenix," he clamped his teeth together as he spoke.

"What's wrong?" They saw that Nick was red in the face with sweat pouring from his forehead.

"Go get Uncle Wrek," he moaned in pain. "This freakin hurts." He was holding onto his knee.

"Why not Mom?"

"Whoever—just keep quiet about the mirror."

Travis unlocked the garage door and went for his Uncle Wrek while Nathan went to the hose for a drink of water.

Wrek hurried to the garage where he entered and knelt beside his nephew.

Nick sat up. "Where's Mom?"

"She's tending to Ian," he replied as he helped him push his pant leg up. "It's swollen, you'll need some ice." He thought. "Better yet, you need an x-ray."

"Just help me to my room."

"You need to go to the hospital!" He peered at Nick.

Nick looked at him. "You know whose fault this is? Paul's." He explained his mishap while Wrek assisted him to his feet.

"I wonder why he was in Nisa's neighborhood?"

Wrek took an ice pack to Nick while Dominique went to the medicine cabinet for some pain reliever. She upped the staircase and when she came to Nick's bedroom door, she overheard whispers of Nathan and Travis' adventure. She opened the door. "Well, that sure was interesting." She looked at her brother as she stepped forward. "The mirror took them to our sister's house, huh?"

"I just heard about it Dom," he defended himself.

She cast her eyes to her son who was sitting on his bed. "What else should I know?"

"Nothing."

She handed the pills to him and exited his room.

"Shit!" Wrek whispered, "You should just tell her."

Dominique and Matt postponed her surprise party for a day or so until everyone felt better.

"What was their excuse?" Matt asked of her while they discussed the boys' adventure within their own bedroom.

"Travis said it was Nathan's idea."

There was a knock.

"Come in," Dominique spoke.

Wrek opened the door and popped his head in. "Can we talk now?"

She waved him in.

He closed the door and with his clean white socks, he walked across her plush blue carpeting. He sat in her oaken wood rocking chair and displayed a fat doober.

"Light it up," Matt suggested before he inserted a game into his console.

Wrek inhaled, then passed the joint to Dominique.

"So what did you want to talk about?" She prepared to listen intently.

He was apprehensive. "Nisa might be in trouble." He bit on his fingernail.

"How?"

Matt pressed the pause button on his controller, then smoked on the reefer as he listened to his brother-in-law.

"She's been getting crank calls and she received a letter in the mail yesterday saying that if she doesn't come up with some money, she would be sorry."

"Wow. This is something you only hear about on TV." She lifted her legs up to her bed and sat Indian style. "How much does she have to have?"

"Fifty thousand," he answered, hoping she would volunteer the ransom.

"Damn!" Matt stated, "That's a lot of dough."

"Who's blackmailing her?" Dominique questioned.

"I don't know for sure, but I have a hunch it's Paul."

"Why don't she call the cops?"

"She's scared. Paul already hurt her once."

"What is she going to do?" She took a hit from the joint and passed it.

"Well . . . that's where my question comes in." He displayed sad eyes and stuck out his lower lip.

"Oh man!" She arose from her bed and paced. "You want me to pay the fifty thousand, huh?" She looked at her brother.

Wrek was hesitant to answer, but exigent with his request.

"I'm gonna have to think about this."

"I'm going to go see her tomorrow." He stood upright from the chair and started for the door.

"Can you show us the letter?" Matt asked.

"Tomorrow. Nisa has it." He left the bedroom.

After checking on her injured, sick, and disobedient sons, Dominique returned to her bedroom where she dimmed the light and locked the door. She walked to her bureau, undressed down to her panties, and as she slipped a nightgown over her head, she observed Matt watching her. "What?" she bantered, then let the garment drop into place.

He gestured for her to draw near as he exhibited a look of want.

"You're going to rub my back?" She laid onto the bed.

"I'll rub something," he replied as he again paused his game.

ELEVEN

COME BY FOR A PARTY

Dominique awoke early the next day in a happy, but troubled mood. Her thoughts were of Wrek's question from the night before. She sat up and moved her hair away from her eyes. She felt the coolness of the morning upon her bare skin and looked downward to see her protruding nipples. She brought a smile to her face as she remembered her and Matt's love making just hours before. As she rolled over and grabbed a cigarette, she read that the time was three thirty. When she flicked the lighter, she heard Matt awaking.

"Come back to bed woman," he whispered.

"I have to go check on Ian first."

Dominique gave her son a dose of medicine and a drink of chocolate milk before kissing him upon his warm forehead. She sat with him until he returned to dreamland. She quietly peeked in on the older boys, then tiptoed down the staircase and back to her own bedroom. Matt had returned to sleep as well.

She looked at the clock to see that the minute hand had circled to the twelve. She took a joint from her night table's drawer and lit it as she walked to the bathroom where she started a bath. As she sat within the bubbles, a thought burst into her mind. "I know what I'm going to do!"

Eight A.M. arrived. Dominique again ascended from her bed, then threw on some casual wear before jaunting into the kitchen. She took a package of sausage and the milk and eggs from the refrigerator and blended the dairy products into a flour mixture. After she plugged in the waffle iron, Wrek entered in.

"Hey Dom, you need any help?"

"Yea." She pointed to the meat. "Fry up those links."

Nick descended the stairs, taking each step slowly. He was outfitted in a designer t-shirt, jean shorts, and white dressing about his patella region. His face displayed pain as he limped to the dinette and positioned himself onto the nearest chair.

"How's the knee?" Dominique asked her son as she carried the platter of waffles from the kitchen. Wrek followed with the sausage and orange juice.

"Hurts."

Ian came dashing into the room with Travis and Nathan trailing. His complexion was restored to his natural color. "Mommy! I'm only a little bit hungry," he spoke as he climbed up to his booster chair.

"I understand. You've been a sick little camper."

His mouth parted and he brought his brows together. "I wasn't camping."

The family laughed.

"It's only an expression Sweetie." She joined them at the preset table, then Wrek spoke a short prayer. Everyone took portions when the food was passed to them. Dominique cut Ian's waffle and poured his juice.

Nick glanced around as he chewed and swallowed. "Did you just sniff that waffle?" he asked his brother with a taunting chuckle in his voice.

Travis set the crisp cake back onto his plate. "So . . . It smells good."

The rest of the kinfolk smiled.

A few minutes had gone by when the discussion of church was brought up.

"I want to go," Dominique replied, "But Ian's still recuperating and perhaps Nick should go to the hospital."

"I'll take him," Matt offered.

"Yea," Nick agreed, wanting to get out of going to church. "It still hurts a lot."

"Can I watch a movie Mama?"

She nodded to Ian.

After breakfast, Wrek went into the garage and stood in front of the full length mirror. As he savored a joint, he blew the smoke onto the reflector. Using the tip of his shoe, he toyed with an oil spill on the cement floor before being taken through the green atmosphere to Phoenix.

"What the hell? This is a first," he spoke as he noticed he was sitting on a limb within a large shade tree.

"What are you doing up there Mister?"

Wrek cast his eyes downward to the voice and saw a small boy. "Uh . . . I'm a detective," he answered as he searched for a branch to step on.

"Are you spying on someone?"

"Yea, so run along so you don't blow my cover." As he watched the child run off, he thought of Zacchaeus who had climbed a sycamore tree to see Jesus. Wrek scanned the area and advanced to a branch before jumping to the ground. He lit a cigarette and walked a few blocks toward Nisa's.

He knocked on the door.

It soon opened. Nisa expressed a nervous, but pleasant smile.

He grinned. "Mmm, you look great in that mini skirt." He observed her appearance as he stepped in and kissed her on the cheek.

She closed the door.

"We need to talk."

"Let's go into the greenhouse." She led the way through the kitchen where she grabbed a few cold beers.

After they entered the room, he again asked her if she'd been in contact with Paul, then he cocked an eye.

She felt irritation in the pit of her stomach. "No."

"He's been seen in this neighborhood."

She thought, for she also wanted to know his facts or proof. "Why do you say that? Have you been gumshoeing?" She sat down on the edge of the daybed.

He chuckled. "No, I haven't been spying." He seated himself next to her and explained his nephew's adventure. He looked at her with wanton as he reached up and gently pulled on her soft curls.

After Nisa lit a tobacco stick, she drew an envelope from her skirt pocket and handed it to Wrek. "Someone slipped this under the front door." Her pink lips didn't speak the truth. "It says to leave the money at Lucy's department store tomorrow at two o'clock."

"It is Paul!" Wrek vented as he drew his brows together. He opened the envelope and read it. The letter was pasted with cut words from a magazine just as the first extortion note was.

"Did you talk to your sister yet about the money?"

"Yea. She doesn't really want to part with the money, but she said she would. She can't get the cash until tomorrow morning." He set the letter down on the bed and leaned in for a kiss. "Come home with me for the rest of the day."

"I've never been through the mirror." Her voice rang of worry.

"It won't hurt," he claimed, "It all happens so quickly. Things turn fuzzy for a second, then it gets dark and then fuzzy again. Before you know it, you're at your destination."

Matt was smoking a bowl when Wrek and Nisa emerged through together.

"That was awesome," she spoke as she viewed her hands and body. She then looked at the conveyor. "Oh . . . This is a beautiful mirror." She reached out and caressed it. "But it's in the garage?"

"Dominique doesn't want it in the house anymore."

Wrek lit a cigarette. "Where's the family?" he asked Matt.

"Dominique's in the kitchen, Nick's resting his knee. The doctor gave him some pain killers." He then offered the pipe to Nisa.

"He's probably feeling real good about now," Wrek commented of Nick and his medicine.

Matt nodded.

"Where's the little guy?" Nisa entreated.

"Ian? He's watching a movie and crying."

"Huh?" she questioned as she looked at Matt.

"He's watching Herbie Goes Bananas. He gets sad when the captain of the ship forces Ocho into the sea."

"That is so sweet." She took a hit and gave the pipe to Wrek.

"Well, I'm done," Matt announced, "I'm going into the house."

Wrek pulled the two coercionary letters from his pocket and handed them to his brother-in-law.

Matt walked toward the door.

"We'll be in shortly."

As he walked into the house, he studied the notes. He entered the kitchen and let the letters fall onto the counter in Dominique's view. "Wrek said she received another one under her front door during the night."

She stopped what she was doing and examined them. "Yeap. This one says exactly what Wrek said it did."

Matt smelled the air. "What are you baking?"

"Banana bread. Ian's request." She looked into his bloodshot eyes. "Wow! You're ripped."

An hour past by when everyone, except Dominique, assembled into the living room. Ian arranged the few gifts upon the coffee table and Nathan distributed confetti to his brothers, uncle, and Nisa.

"Okay guys. I'll go get your mom," Matt spoke.

"Hide everyone!" Ian suggested.

When Matt entered his bedroom, Dominique was curled up upon the bed. "Are you sleeping?" he whispered as he sat beside her.

"No, just resting. I think I'm premenstrual."

"Eww . . ."

"I took some ibuprofen a bit ago." She lifted her head slightly to look at him.

"Do you feel like visiting with Wrek and Nisa?"

She sighed. "I suppose so."

There was a knock at the front door. Nick who was standing near, opened it. "Hey . . . Dash right?"

"Yea. Is Matt here? He said to come by for a birthday party."

"Come on in." He widened the gap. "We're getting ready to throw the confetti."

The group eyed the stranger as he walked in. Nathan quickly stepped to him and poured some of the small pieces of colored paper into his cupped hands.

Matt and Dominique entered the room.

"Surprise!" Everyone yelled as they threw the confetti into the air toward her.

"Oh wow. This is great!"

Ian hopped to her and wrapped his lean arms around her thigh. "Happy Birthday Mama."

Dash watched her with promiscuous eyes. He studied her every curve and line.

There was small talk among the group while Matt and Dominique advanced to the love seat. Dash sat onto a cheap metal chair next to Nick while Wrek sat close to Nisa on the couch. Ian roamed about the coffee table, aching to hand presents to his mom.

Matt spoke to Dash as he lit a cigarette. "Have you met my brother-in-law, Wrek?"

"No." He turned to Wrek. "But it's nice to meet you."

Matt then pointed to Nisa. "This is his girlfriend."

Dash scanned her facial features. "Is she your sister or cousin?"

"No," Matt replied, "Why do you say that?"

"She looks like you."

"How?" He lowered his brow with curiosity.

"You two have the same shape of eyebrows and forehead."

"And they both have black hair," Ian inserted.

"Hmm. No, I only met her a few months ago."

Dominique opened one of her presents. It was a sketch of a shoe within a glass frame. "Oh . . . I love it. Thank you Ian." She showed it to everyone.

Matt took hold of it. "This is a good drawing for a five year old."

Wrek stood and walked to the kitchen. Dominique and two of her sons followed. Travis took hold of the birthday cake while Nathan gathered plates and forks. Dominique carried the knife; Wrek grabbed four beers.

Moments later, they all joined in the dining room. Wrek gave a beer to Dash, one to Matt, and two for himself and Nisa.

"So—Matt," Wrek mingled, "Where did you and Dash meet?"

"We were cell mates."

"Yea," Dash boasted, "I blew up a pop machine . . ."

The dark sky settled in and Wrek escorted Nisa through the mirror to her home. The boys scattered to their bedrooms and Dominique went to the bathroom where she changed out of her blouse and bra into a jean vest she just received. The garment left extra arm space that gave view to half of her breasts.

Matt was on his fifth beer and had taken shots from Dash's whiskey bottle. Dominique was persuaded as well to down a shot of the strong drink, but only with a cola chaser.

Dash was having a good time with his new friend and reminiscing with Matt. He took it easy on his drinking, for he wanted Matt to be drunker than him. While they talked, he copped as many peeks as he could of Dominique's units.

Soon Matt arose and staggered to the bathroom. When he did, Dominique also ascended. She circled the house, shutting off lights and all the while, her mental activity was that of Dash. She thought he was sexy for a man of forty-five with blue eyes and advanced wrinkles. His sweet charm and sly comments stirred her insides; something that she knew only Matt should be doing, but rarely gave the effort anymore.

Matt was seen wobbling into his bedroom by Dominique who followed and noted that he was lying face down on the bed. She stepped to him and leaned in. "Matt?"

He mumbled that he was drunk and for her to send Dash away. He lay motionless.

She switched off the light and returned to the living room. She lit a cigarette and cast a peek at Dash who had just came in from outside.

"Did Matt go to bed?"

She nodded. "He wants you to leave."

Using Matt's absence, Dash stepped to where she stood and spoke low. "But first, I have something sweet for you to suck on." He gently secured her hand and placed a lollipop into it. "Happy Birthday." He beheld her pose as he waited for her reaction.

Her eyes held a hint of embarrassment. She smiled and ignored his statement.

He wore a sexy smile on his face as he stepped to her side, then rounded about her backside to her other side.

As she puffed on her cigarette, she observed out of the corner of her eye, his silent stare as he strolled within her view. He encircled again, this time his lips were puckered slightly as though he was lusting over her hot body. He let one of his hands swipe across her ass.

The unexpected touch startled her, yet she felt as though she could melt from his brush. Still, she stepped away.

Dash's play for her was cut short when they heard the back door come into use, then Wrek ascended into the room.

TWELVE

THE DROP

WHEN DOMINIQUE AWOKE, she thought about the night before; the awkward comments Dash had planted into her mind as they shared a closeness with their bodies.

Her head ached. She sat up, lit a cigarette, and rotated to catch a peek at Matt. He was still sleeping and she could smell his rank morning breath. She arose and headed for the window. She guided the pane open and as she scanned the neighborhood, she blew her smoke through the gap and sometimes, the wind returned the fumes.

The pumpkins and decorations of ghosts and gobblins made it apparent of the autumn season. She watched the fallen leaves scatter across the yard and down the street.

It was going to be a busy Monday. After taking a few pain killers and a shower, she awoke Matt and went to the kitchen for a light breakfast. She then trodded upstairs to rouse the boys for school. Soon they were on their way.

Dominique, Matt, and Ian cruised to the post office, then to a variety store. Ian showed interest in the Halloween adornments as well as all the toys. Dominique selected a few items throughout the store including all the play money from the toy aisle.

Matt observed her selection. "What's your plan woman?"

"My plan?" She looked into his curious green eyes. "I'm definently not going to fork over fifty grand."

"I agree. We need to talk."

They left the store and sat within the car.

"I suggest we stake out this Lucy's Department Store . . ."

"We? I can't go with you." She glanced at her child who was in the backseat. "He can't return to school until tomorrow. You and Wrek will have to do the watching and catch this guy yourselves." She adjusted herself onto the seat and started the engine.

Ian sat in his booster seat and strapped his belt.

Dominique exited from the parking lot and drove to the bank where she withdrew from her savings account, two thousand dollars in hundreds and one dollar bills. She then headed straight home.

Matt and Dominique entered into the house and went to their bedroom while Ian stayed in the living room, took hold and emptied his container of special cars onto his play table in the TV area.

Dominique locked the bedroom door, slid her shoes off as she walked to the bed, then dumped her purchased contents onto the mattress. She sat down and secured the loot from her purse.

Matt joined his wife on the bed and began unwrapping the plastic from the phony money.

"I hope the mirror cooperates for you today." She took hold of a pile of the fake money and placed a Franklin on each end.

"We'll just take a few quick tokes and tell it that Nisa needs our help for the rest of the day."

"You don't have to smoke to activate it. Ian and I went though it sober."

He considered her statement and reflected on the mirror's reasons.

She twisted a rubber band around the first stack and displayed it. "Looks feasible, huh?"

He looked at it then at her. "What do you think motivates the mirror?"

"Nisa."

She put the bound cash into a brown paper bag and gave Matt an extra three hundred for expenses. "Good luck at catching this guy." She leaned in and kissed his lips. "If you do confront Paul in public, maybe he will leave Nisa alone."

They went to the kitchen where Wrek and Nick were snacking. Dominique stood in the doorway, puffing on a cigarette. Matt stepped to Wrek and pointed to the paper bag. "It's all here. Are you ready to go do some detective work?"

"Sure am," he answered, then turned to Nick. "You want to hide in the parking lot and keep an eye out for Paul's truck?"

"Hell no!" he quickly replied.

Wrek chuckled while Dominique frowned on her son's language.

"He can barely walk," Matt concluded.

"I'll go then," Dominique spoke, "Nick can watch Ian."

Matt was pleased that she would be accompanying him.

She dispensed a dose of medicine to Ian, then applied a good bye kiss to his forehead and left him in Nick's care. She followed her husband and brother to the garage. Wrek closed the door and as he went to the mirror, he lit a joint. They stood in front of the reflector and Wrek began to caress and talk to it. The air became virescent.

In Phoenix, the trio arrived at Nisa's door and they were quickly invited in. Everyone was wearing sneakers with blue jeans except for Nisa. She wore moccasins.

Wrek stepped in and wrapped his arms around her tiny body. "My beautiful minikin," he whispered into her ear.

"I received another letter under the door," she spoke faint.

"Let's see it."

Matt and Dominique watched the exhibit of emotion and the opening of the envelope. "What's it say?" They stepped in while Nisa closed the entry door.

"It says," he read, "Nisa is to buy a black briefcase at Lucy's, put the money in it, and leave it in the middle booth in the ladies' dressing room."

"Hmm," Dominique hummed.

"I wonder why the ladies' room?" Matt questioned as he pulled a cigarette from his pack.

"He has to have a female partner," Nisa suggested.

"Maybe even one of the employees," Dominique added.

"Well," Matt said, "I'll be in the store and I'll see what happens."

Dominique went to the telephone and after looking up a number, she dialed for a taxi.

Some ten minutes later and the group was on their way to the mall, to Lucy's Department Store.

As they rode, Nisa worried about her plan. She knew if she didn't get away with the money, Matt and Dominique would keep it and perhaps keep it forever.

Wrek and Nisa held hands as they walked precedent to the two generous victims upon the mall floor until they came to the entrance of the elegant clothing and luggage store. Across the way, was the food court.

"Wrek. You and Nisa go wait at a table while Dominique and I check things out in the store. Paul knows who three of us look like, so lay low." He took from his pocket, a twenty dollar bill and handed it to his brother-in-law. "Get some lunch."

The food court was crowded as they stood in line at the Mexican counter. Wrek scanned the area. He saw all the usual mall décor: Retail stores, signs, benches, artificial trees, and people. He then noted Nisa's visual observations and smiled. "Why are you eyeing me?"

She took hold of his arm and spoke sensuously. "I don't have a pet name for you yet."

He looked away and as he thought, he glanced at one of those fake trees and remembered. "Just call me Zacchaeus." He puffed out his chest.

She carried an odd look upon her face. "Who's Zacch . . . whoever you said?"

"You don't know Zacchaeus?"

She replied with a no.

"He was the wee little man who climbed a sycamore tree to see Jesus."

"Why'd he do that?"

"There was a crowd of people. He couldn't see."

"Sounds like he was a smart guy, but why should I call you Zacchaeus?"

They ordered their food, then after obtaining a table, he explained to her, how a few days ago, the mirror landed him on a branch.

Matt and Dominique investigated the layout of Lucy's Department Store and its changing rooms before heading out.

"There's an exit door in the back by the dressing rooms," she informed her husband. "It has an alarm, so it will sound if anyone goes out of it."

"Or in." He looked at his watch. "Twelve fifty. We have an hour."

"Good. I'm going to get some lunch."

They joined Wrek and Nisa at their table where they talked and ate. Matt assigned positions, then went for a cigarette break at the nearest outside door.

One fifty-five was upon them and Dominique was walking the blacktop searching for the old brown clunker, with or without a camper, while Wrek minded his post from the food court. With a shopping bag in hand, Nisa followed Matt into Lucy's Department Store and they both casually glanced and thumbed a few items from a clearance rack.

A few more ticks of the clock and Nisa ambled toward the women's clothing to browse while Matt went straightway to the luggage section where he quickly chose a briefcase. He walked to a counter and as he handed some cash to the cashier, he held himself stern and quiet. His heart was adjusting to the thrill of spying and he wondered and thought about what he would say to Paul.

The clerk slipped his black portfolio into a shopping bag, then gave him the receipt and change. "Thank you," she bid, "Come again."

Matt turned away and carried his shopping bag with him. He went to the menswear and delayed himself at a clothing rack while he took hold of two shirts. He then walked through an extravagant lobby towards the men's dressing rooms.

He selected a booth and after entering, he shut and locked the wooden door. He hung the garments onto a curved hook. "Fancy, are we?" he spoke when he noticed the device was gold-plated. He set the bag onto the floor and pulled the briefcase out, then opened and placed it on the bench.

Nisa's anticipation grew as she flipped through dresses and skirts. She thought it was rather boring to do so, knowing she wasn't going to buy anything. She cast her eyes about, hoping for Matt to appear. She would then inconspicuously take the money filled briefcase and pretend to leave it in the middle booth for Paul. She drew a deep breath and forced her muscles to relax.

Another minute and Matt stepped to the metal framework of clothes where Nisa stood. He rested his paper sack atop of the floor next to Nisa's barren shopping bag and gave his attention to browsing.

Nisa took hold of two dresses, bent down and secured her hand onto Matt's paper receptacle, then walked off.

Matt assumed Nisa's weightless bag and as he wandered about the men's clothing, he patiently waited for Nisa to make the quick drop. He observed the shoppers and saw a male employee who was straightening miscellaneous items near the entry of the store. "Excellent," he mumbled.

In the middle booth, Nisa fixed the dresses onto a shiny hook and recovered a plastic bag hidden within her bra. She set the briefcase upon the hardwood bench. Her hands were sweaty and she couldn't stop shaking; she was anxious to see her fifty grand.

As she picked up a packet of money, she emitted a grin. With her thumb, she flipped through the bills seeing the phony money. "Damn it," she whispered, then checked another bundle.

With great disappointment, she seized the remaining packets and stuffed them into her synthetic bag. Curiosity made her look in the upper compartment of the case. She was disturbed when she saw a clothes detector.

Wrek kept the entry way of Lucy's under surveillance as he paced the food court and corridor. Soon his probing directed him to peek down the maintenance hall that led to a janitor's closet and the bathrooms. Within the minute, he returned to the lunch room and waited for Nisa.

Dominique went about the parking lots searching for the perpetrator's truck. She checked the north and east parking areas, patrolling and circling through the rows. In the south lot, after walking between two cars, a security guard approached her.

"Do you need help finding your car?" he asked after seeing her suspicious wandering.

"No."

"What are you doing then?"

"I am looking for my car," she fabricated, "but I don't need any help." With that, she walked away feeling his eyes upon her.

Nisa stepped out of the booth to the large mirror on the wall and stood. She glanced to her left, then to her right. With no one around, she tossed the bag of money into the garbage can and returned to the small cubicle with an idea.

She clutched onto a detector from a dress and pulled until it tore away. She quickly did the same to the other dress, then with the three devices, she left the booth. As she walked past the first booth, she noticed a shopping bag that was upon the floor just inside the booth. She slipped a detector into the paper container, then rounded the corner and did the same to another shopping bag. She exited the dressing room area and using more stealth, she placed the third detector into a shopping bag that a woman carried.

Matt kept his attention toward the dressing rooms when he wasn't being inconvenienced by the sales clerk or by another shopper who wanted to complain about the prices.

Nisa wasted no time leaving the woman's department and crossing the walkway towards Matt.

"What took you so long?" he vented as he kept browsing.

"There was someone in that booth," she stressed, "I had to wait."

"Okay." He softened his tone. "Go wait in the food court."

Nisa left the men's department, but not the store. She stood out of sight in back of a rack of clothes and spied on Matt, the nearby cashier, and the store entry. She crept to another rack, then across the walkway to the woman's section. She froze behind a stand of shirts when she heard the theft alarm sound.

Matt stepped to the store's entrance and witnessed a security guard checking the bag of a shopper. The guard extracted a detector and noticed it wasn't attached to any clothing.

"I didn't buy anything in this store," the shopper stated.

The watchman kept the device and the customer left. Matt turned toward the inside of the store and ambled up the walkway.

As Nisa continued to slink toward the dressing rooms, the shoplifters detection system began to beep again. She knew where Matt would be, so she hastened to the lady's dressing room. She reached into the trash can, took hold of the bag of money, and darted out the exit door.

Wrek joined Matt at the entrance and observed a second customer's bag being inspected. At that moment, they heard the ringing from the exit door. Matt dashed to the women's dressing room, by-passed an employee who seemed to be confused by the open door, and tore to the center booth.

"Hey!" the employee called out, "There's no men allowed in here."

Matt pushed on the thin wooden door and entered to see an empty briefcase. "Damn it!" He quickly turned and left the booth, then the establishment through the exit door.

Nisa hurried into the women's mall restroom, to the farthest stall and placed the bag onto the toilet's far side. Her heart was thumping as she gasped for air. She parted her lips to quiet her breathing, then opened the plastic carrier. "I did it!" she whispered to herself as she pulled the first packet out. Soon she had the hundred dollar bills stuffed neatly into her pocket and the play money, she dumped into the garbage can.

Matt rushed through the corridor, then rounded the corner to the store's entrance where Wrek and Dominique awaited. "Nothing," he spoke with disappointment. "Did you see Paul or anyone suspicious?"

"No."

"Well." He looked at his wife. "There went your money."

Wrek cast his eyes about. "Where's Nisa?"

"I sent her out to the food court," Matt replied while they scanned the area. "I need a cigarette."

Nisa repressed her emotions as she neared her boyfriend and her bankers.

"Where were you?" Wrek asked her.

"I was browsing the video store. I thought I saw Paul's old girlfriend, but it wasn't her."

"You had me worried." He took her hand and they followed Matt and Dominique to the parking lot.

Outside the mall, Matt cuffed his hand to block the breeze as he lit a cigarette. He turned to Dominique and Wrek. "I think we should go cruise out to Paul's house."

THIRTEEN

THE NEXT TWO HOURS

"ARE YOU FUCKING serious?" Wrek asked Matt with a look of shock upon his face. "You want to go creeping and crawling around Paul's house?"

"No. I want to go IN his house," he replied, then took a drag from his cigarette.

"Are you crazy? That son of a bitch carries a gun."

"I want to look for evidence."

"And then what?"

Nisa stood listening to their conversation, knowing they wouldn't find anything at Paul's. "Count me out," she stated, "I want to go home."

Dominique approached them after using the pay phone. "The cab is on its way."

Wrek looked at Matt. "We can't take a cab to Paul's."

Matt thought. "We'll have to rent a car."

Soon enough, the yellow cab arrived and they left the mall. The driver offloaded the three sherlocks down the street at a car rental enterprise, then took Nisa home.

Matt and Dominique leased a black sports car. Matt allowed the tires to screech as he accelerated out onto Central

Avenue. Wrek loaded his pipe and let the space in the car fill with the mind altering smoke.

They motored their way due south to Dobbins Road. To the west of them, dark clouds lay at the rim of the city. The airborne mass carried flashes as it slowly moved.

Matt, Dominique, and Wrek were smoking cigarettes as they entered onto the dirt road. When they came to the last tree just before Paul's property, Matt stopped the car. They studied the surroundings and Dominique pointed out the empty driveway.

Matt looked to his right and noted a garage. He recognized the building from before, he just hadn't given it much thought.

"KKKRRR!" was the sound of thunder. The wind was growing stronger as Matt drove to the far side of the garage and parked. He turned to his wife. "You be ready to hightail it out of here if you run into any trouble or when we return. Paul can't see the car from here."

The clouds now covered the sun. The smell of rain was adrift as the two men stepped out of the car. They stood at the edge of the garage and took one last peek before treading to the shabby blue house.

Back in Kellogg, Travis and Nathan were returning home from school. "Where's mom?"

"She ain't home from Phoenix yet," Nick revealed.

"Hmm . . ." Nathan remarked, "How long til she gets home?"

"About an hour."

There was a knock at the rear door. While Nathan hastened to answer it, Travis went upstairs to his bedroom and Ian continued to push his micro cars upon the coffee table. The television echoed voices and sound effects from Ian's selected movie.

Nathan let his friend into the house. They talked of what to do as he gathered ham and cheese snacks from the refrigerator. Sandy grabbed two pops and followed him outside. They zipped their jackets, for the sky was a gray abyss and the temperature gauge on the porch read forty-seven.

Their boredom led them to wander to the outbuilding where the motorized toys were stored.

"Let's go four-wheelin up Wardner," Sandy hinted.

"I'm already grounded again," he stressed. "And besides, I'd have to go sneak the keys out of my mom's room."

"We could stop by my house and be back in forty-five minutes," he coaxed.

Matt and Wrek glanced in through the windows as they passed by. They felt the raindrops upon their curious faces as they neared the entry door. Matt turned the knob. It was unlocked and when he pushed it open, it gave a short squeak. All was hazy and gray, so Matt turned on his newly purchased flashlight and entered with caution.

Wrek switched on his own illuminator and followed. They tiptoed across the kitchen floor and in to the living room. When Matt confirmed his suspicion that Paul wasn't home, he flipped on the hall light. He told Wrek to search for play money and cut-up magazines. Soon they hurried to Paul's bedroom.

They could hear the downpour on the roof. Matt looked through some books on the night table. "We'll probably never retrieve the two grand from him, but . . ."

"What?" Wrek interrupted as he stopped searching in the garbage can and eyed him.

"What what?" Matt questioned.

"You said two grand. I thought you handed over fifty thousand to him?"

"No," Matt explained as they rummaged through the dresser drawers.

The heavy rain pounded onto the windshield. Dominique sat nervous in the driver's seat as she kept the wiperblades running. To her, it seemed as though the lightening was striking a bit too close for comfort.

Visibility was limited. The headlights from Paul's vehicle blended within the flashes and watery mist about his truck as he drove up to his house.

Matt and Wrek became fearful when they heard the sound of a vehicle door being closed. They rushed to the window to see Paul's truck. "Oh fuck me," Wrek blurted.

"Shh . . . Turn off your flashlight!" he whispered.

Their hearts were thumping. They didn't have any weapons with them and they left the hall light on. They wanted to avoid uncertainty with this man, so they remained still.

Paul's footsteps and noises seemed to indicate he was in the kitchen opening a can of beer or soda. They heard the rough clatter of dirty dishes being tossed into the sink before there was silence. They listened more intensely to their suspect's actions. The accent of paper being handled was apparent.

Wrek raised a brow. "Maybe he's counting the money," he spoke under his breath.

As Matt stood against the wall listening, flashbacks of a childhood incident came to mind. He recalled a similar time when his father had hurled some plates about the living room, shooting at them with a BB gun. Stanley was inebriated and his parents had been arguing. Matt and his brother David were peeking around the edge of the corridor when they saw their dad push their mother. Matt remembered storming into the room and expressing his concern. "Don't push her!"

Like a volcanic eruption, Stanley turned to him and spewed his anger. "You want some of this too?" He aimed the BB gun at him and fired.

Matt refocused in on the present and stepped to the window where he quietly tested to see if the pane would slide open. He had it at an inch when he became aware of Paul walking towards the bedroom. They had their flashlights ready to strike, but then they saw the bathroom light go on and the door move to a near close. They exhaled.

"Come on," Matt lipped.

Matt and Wrek heard moans of passion coming from Paul as they snuck towards the bedroom door to exit. They ached having to tiptoe past the partly open door and as they did, they both caught a glimpse of their culprit slowly stroking his erected penis over the counter. Matt made a sour face as he mentally rebuked himself for looking.

They entered the kitchen and there sat atop of the table, a smutty magazine. Matt noted the open page, but left it alone. He didn't want to thumb through what Paul had touched. However, Wrek snagged it.

The two slinks exited the house. Wrek rolled and stuck his obscene literature under his sweat shirt as he ran parallel with Matt across the mud. A rainbow was manifested throughout the northern end of the sky as they rounded the garage and climbed into the rental car.

"Let's go."

Dominique had the engine running and the heater set on the defrost to clear the steam. As she drove away, she noticed Paul's truck in the driveway and was amazed she didn't see it arriving in spite of the sudden and quick storm.

The rain was null as they traveled upon the puddly road. Matt dabbed his forehead of wetness, then lit a cigarette. "We didn't find a thing," he told his wife.

Wrek poked his head in between the two front seats. "I'm worried about Nisa. If Paul only got two thousand, he's still going to want the rest of his money."

"Maybe." He took a drag from his tobacco stick. "I thought perhaps we could of caught him walking out of the store with the briefcase."

Dominique glanced at her husband. "You told him?"

He nodded.

"Sounds like you two had it all planned out." Wrek's attitude hinted of jealousy.

"We're not even one hundred percent sure it's Paul wanting the fifty grand," Matt spoke as he turned to his brother-in-law, then directed his wife to make a left turn onto Central Avenue.

"Who else would want your money?"

There was silence.

"You don't suspect Nisa, do you?" Wrek complained.

"I don't know," Matt concluded.

Matt and Wrek waited in the parking lot of the rental store while Dominique checked the car in and returned the key. She turned to leave the building and as she approached the exit door, she saw a green cloud.

"Thank you Ma'am," the attendant spoke, then looked up to see an empty room. "Where'd she go?" He wondered as he cast his eyes about.

A moment after Dominique was uprooted through the mirror to her estate in Kellogg, Matt and Wrek arrived. She lit a cigarette and stepped from the garage to the back lawn. The sun was disappearing behind the mountain and an October chill was in the air. She scanned her yard, then saw the automatic door on the outbuilding was open. She hastened to the shed and noticed that her and Matt's three all-terrain vehicles had been jacked.

Matt stepped in behind her. "Weren't they grounded?"

"Yes they were. Three of them this time." She went to her house, inside to the rear entry, and when she was putting on her jacket, she heard the engines of her missing vehicles. She returned to the shed carrying Matt's black trench coat. She poked her attention to the dirt path and viewed two of the ATV'S approaching with her boys. Where was her third vehicle?

Travis and Nathan parked and cut the engines. Dominique, Matt, and Wrek stood with their arms crossed waiting for answers.

"Mom," Travis spoke low as he lifted his head and observed a scowl upon her face. "I wrecked the blue four-wheeler."

"Are you okay?" she asked, suppressing her anger.

He nodded. "I didn't mean to wreck it . . ."

Matt interrupted. "Who snuck the keys from our bedroom?"

At that moment, the sound of a pindrop could have been heard throughout the outbuilding, then Nathan confessed.

"Who's idea was this?"

"What's it matter?" Wrek cut in. "They're all guilty."

Dominique glared at her pirates.

"Sandy," one answered.

She looked at Nathan and spoke. "You could of said, 'No Sandy, go home!'" She then ordered them both into the house with a snap of her finger and the pointing of her arm. She trekked in after them, tossed her jacket onto a hook, and as they entered the kitchen, she continued to scold, commanding them to get upstairs to their rooms.

"We're going." Travis sassed as he turned and sent a glare her way.

Thoughts of his rudeness and persnickety attitude came to mind, making her insides boil. She stepped forward and grabbed the back of his sweater, turned him around and slapped upon his head and face. In the midst of her unrestraint action, she delivered a closed fist to his mouth as Nathan watched in horror, wondering what to do.

Dominique quickly switched to Nathan, giving him a dose of slaps. She stopped. Her breathing was rapid as she returned her visual perception to Travis and observed a small amount of blood on his lip. Her heart sank; she felt awful. It had happened so fast, she couldn't believe what she had just done. "I'm sorry Travis." She left and went to her bedroom.

Nathan rubbed his sore cheek. "Come on Travis, we deserved it," he spoke as he turned and headed upstairs.

"Speak for yourself. I just went along for the ride that you talked me into doing."

Matt locked the shed and with his brother-in-law's help, they carried the cheval mirror from the garage to the house.

"Is Dominique okay with this?" Wrek questioned.

"Yea, but we have to face the glass toward the wall."

Dominique had changed her clothes and was sitting on her antique restauration sofa when she heard a quiet knock on the lower part of her bedroom door. She presumed it was her youngest. "Come in." She dabbed her watery eyes with a tissue.

Ian entered. "Mommy?"

She held her arms out for him. "Come here Baby Zebra." Her speech pattern was that of baby talk.

He carried his orange stitched tiger as he hurried across the room and jumped onto her lap. He set his sights upon her face and saw that she'd been crying. "Did you beat up Travis and Nathan?"

She cracked a soft smile. "No, I didn't beat them up." She held him close to her afflicted heart and kissed him. "Are you hungry?"

"Yea . . . and so is Duhe." He was looking down as he fiddled with the toy's ear.

"You need a dose of medicine anyways." She put him off her lap and as she stood, she yawned. "Oh goodness. It's to bed early tonight."

In the kitchen, Nick limped across the floor towards his mom who was dispensing liquid antibiotics to Ian. He took hold of his prescribed pain killers that were distributed onto the counter top and swallowed them with no water.

Dominique looked at the clock and noted the first evening hour. "Would you go tell your brothers to shower and come down for dinner," she spoke to Nick as she pinpointed the telephone number for pizza delivery, then dialed.

Some ten minutes later, Nathan who wore a white t-shirt with sports shorts, descended from his bedroom to the bottom of the staircase. As he entered the living room, he looked with caution at his mother.

Dominique's face sported a welcoming grin as she talked of the insurance and how Matt and Wrek would go retrieve the four-wheeler tomorrow.

"I have homework."

"What kind?" she asked.

"Math, social studies, and reading questions." He displayed a feel sorry for me look as he awaited her answer.

"I'll do your social studies." She gave him a hug then headed up the stairway to befriend Travis once again.

FOURTEEN

TRICK OR TREAT

"TRICK OR TREAT, smell my feet." That was the talk of the dark and ghostly neighborhood. The air was nippy as the undersized frankensteins, vampires, and princesses walked door to door. Ian went at a fast pace over the lawns and sidewalks while Dominique followed and waited at the edge of the street with Wrek.

Matt stayed at home and while he handed out candy to the knockers, he wore a gruesome monster mask to enhance the thrill.

Ian's bag was weighing him down so Dominique gave him the emergency bag, then took and carried his first collection.

Wrek lit a cigarette as he watched a small child struggle with her costume. He turned to his sister. "Remember when you were a cornbread for Halloween?"

She grinned as she pictured her upper torso in that yellow crete papered cardboard box running from house to house. Her arms, she recalled, were poking out the side holes and it was cumbersome as she carried the bag of candy. "I was about ten years old then. I remember ditching that thing next to a garbage can on the way home."

Travis, Nathan, and Sandy each carried six eggs and a roll of toilet paper. They considered themselves too mature to go begging for sweet confection, instead, they wanted to take part in some mischief.

The three capers walked among a few of the trick or treaters on McKinley Avenue. Sandy watched as two little girls dressed as cats, acknowledged their plump mothers who kept an eye on them from the street. Soon the guys passed by the women and as they did, they gave a nod and a brief hello.

The two feline panhandlers were upon a private walkway, nearing the main sidewalk. Sandy brought his head close in to Nathan's. "Get ready to run."

"Huh?" he questioned.

Through the darkness, Sandy scampered up to the girls and snatched a bag of candy, then ran.

"Hey!" the victim cried out, "That's my candy." She gyrated. "Mom?"

"Oh shit!" Nathan took off running in the direction of his friend.

Travis observed the theft and as he dashed away silently, a few eggs fell from his jacket pocket. One landed and broke atop of his clean shoe. "Dang it!"

The three juveniles hastened up a short inclined side street, then zipped through an alley. They were breathing hard when they turned themselves around and glanced aback. They rounded the brick building and slowed to a walk.

"Whad you do that for?" Travis complained with a frown as he looked to Sandy.

"I got us some free candy." He stopped and held the bag out for show.

"We're only off grounded for two hours," he stressed, "If we get caught doing anything wrong, our mom will take away our four-wheelers and sell them."

"Maybe you should go home then."

Travis clutched his fist.

Sandy cast his persuasive eyes upon Nathan. "We each agreed to do something tonight."

"Pranks, not crimes."

"And it's your turn," he declared.

Travis suppressed his anger as they ventured south on Main Street. Nathan scanned the area; it was quiet. An unoccupied police car was parked parallel to the sidewalk in front of the police station.

Ian had stopped his trick or treating momentarily to ogle over a scarecrow and some unique decorations. Dominique puffed on a cigarette as she watched her son. She and her brother were bundled well within their jackets and stocking hats. Her breath was as steam when she talked. "Wrek, I want to tell you something, but you can't tell Matt."

"I won't." He pulled his loaded pipe from his pocket.

Dominique let her cigarette drop to the pavement and as she stepped on the cherry, she heard Ian screaming. She cast her eyes upon him and noticed the scarecrow had come to life. Ian who had terror emitting from his face, came running. She knelt and embraced her son. "It's only a man dressed like a scarecrow Sweetie," she explained.

Wrek chuckled.

Ian looked up at his uncle through the darkness. "Stop laughing at me!"

Soon Dominique and Wrek were watching Ian race across a lawn to join other kids at a door.

"You were going to tell me something," Wrek reminded his sister.

"Yea . . ." she paused. "Dash wants me."

"He'd better not! You're married."

She giggled at his seriousness.

Wrek thought a moment as he toked. "Do you want him?"

Dominique shifted her scarf upward and over her mouth, leaving her eyes and red nose to the bitter air. "I like his flirting." There was a silent delay. "I don't know if I could bring myself to do anything with him or not. I'd feel guilty."

"Good." He handed his metal smoker to her.

"I'm sure tempted though," she remarked as she glanced at him.

Wrek gazed up at the night sky and noted a few snowflakes landing upon his face. "I'm glad I finally found someone," he spoke, then opened his mouth to let some of the falling ice crystals wet his tongue.

"Yea, I'm happy for you." She pulled her scarf down from her mouth and enjoyed also, the drops of coldness touching upon her lips and face.

Wrek brought his head down. "I think I love her," he admitted to his sister, then took hold of his illegal device. "I'm thinking about moving to Phoenix; maybe share an apartment with her."

"Does she want to shack up with you?"

"I haven't asked her yet."

Ian administered his last holiday knock and collected his final treat. He and his two lookouts didn't have far to walk; they were close to home.

Inside the house, Ian quickly tossed his jacket and boots to the carpet, then dumped his bags of candy into a pile on the floor. He sat with his legs extended out and about his heap, then he began to set each piece into its appropriate stack.

Dominique looked at her watch. "They have twenty minutes left."

Travis and Nathan held eggs within their hands as they dared to near the police car. They took a glimpse at the door and windows of the law enforcement building, then with selfish motives, they pegged the patrol car with their raw ammunition. Broken shells and yolk oozed down the windshield and the logo on the door was clouded.

Sandy took his roll of toilet paper and let it uncoil as he ran around the car. He then followed Travis and Nathan who took off running upon the sidewalk towards the four-way stop and past a bank where they ducked into an alley.

"That was awesome!" Nathan exclaimed as they panted for air.

They continued to journey behind a few buildings before resurfacing onto McKinley Avenue. They were cavorting and throwing eggs at the windows of businesses as they headed for the grandstand.

Travis, Nathan, and Sandy neared an entrance gate. "Last one down wants to kiss Jenny Kay," Sandy instigated, so they trampled down the steps, grabbing and pulling onto each others arms and jacket collars.

They soon calmed down as they walked across the empty football field snacking on Sandy's stolen candy. The town was void of young trick or treaters when they crossed Hill Street and directed themselves to the city park. They went through the parking lot and past the swimming pool. Out of curiosity, Travis tossed his last egg into the water to hear the mild plop.

The vandals rid themselves of any evidence by tossing the rolled paper again and again over the swing set and slide. A glimpse from a pair of headlights caught their attention when a squad car entered the lot with its searchlight aglow. The two brothers scampered away toward the motel while Sandy ran around the fenced pool.

The officer leaped from his car and gave chase to Sandy who raced off into the darkness toward the cement stairway. He was part way up the flight of steps when the cop grabbed his ankle and yelled for him to stop resisting.

Travis and Nathan spied Sandy's capture from a dark street corner.

"You think he'll rat us out?" Travis asked his younger brother.

"Na. I think he'll keep quiet." They turned and hastened for home.

Dominique was standing in the midst of her living room watching Ian pile his Halloween candy into a large mixing bowl when Travis and Nathan came into the house.

"Hi Mom!" they shouted as they darted up the steps to their bedrooms. Travis kicked off his egg soiled sneakers and paced within his room while his heart thumped of guilt. Nathan took off his jacket and sat on the edge of his bed, wondering how much trouble his friend was in.

Dominique hopped the staircase and knocked on Travis' door. She entered and observed his crisp, but pale complexion.

When Nathan heard his mom's voice, he stood and crept to his door where he listened in on her and Travis' words.

"I'll keep quiet, but if the cops show up at our front door, you two are going to fess up to it."

He was relieved as he stepped into Travis' room. "How can we find out about Sandy?" he questioned his mother as he stood beside the dresser drawers.

"Call him tomorrow. If he's not there, maybe his mom will tell you."

"Or she'll question you," Travis added.

He thought. "Maybe I'll just wait for him to call me."

Dominique eyed her sons. "Don't you two feel ashamed of what you did?"

There was a pause.

"Yea. I prayed to Jesus to forgive me," Nathan admitted. "It was fun what we did, but I know it was wrong."

She hugged her boys. "I'm going to the kitchen. How many corn dogs do you guys want?"

"Two."

"One plus some curly fries," Travis, the slender one answered.

FIFTEEN

ANOTHER LETTER

A FEW DAYS into November brought a morning newspaper with an article and picture of the vandalism in Kellogg. The report claimed a local juvenile was charged and sent to the detention center.

Nathan ached within his gut as he sank into his chair at the breakfast table. He took a few sips of his orange juice before following Travis and Matt out the exterior door.

The smell of coffee drifted throughout Aunt Penny's kitchen as the percolator gurgled. Nisa entered the room with a yawn and stepped to the coffeepot. She took a cup and when the hot liquid was done brewing, she poured herself a fill. "Mmm . . . That tastes good," she moaned. She set the cup down, went to the refrigerator, and opened the freezer. "What do you want for dinner tonight?" she asked her aunt as she rummaged through the contents.

"Nothing with hamburger," she answered.

Nisa removed a package of pork chops along with another package of meat and set them both in the sink to defrost.

Aunt Penny soon left for work. Nisa rinsed out the old coffeepot and turned on a small radio before sitting at the kitchen table with her scissors and glue. She browsed through some magazines and newspapers. "Two thousand my ass. I want it all!" she grumbled to herself.

With Matt and Wrek at work, Dominique spent the morning writing a scene for her second novel while Ian watched two movies and played with his small metal cars. The time was approaching eleven when she set her pen down and went into the kitchen for a little lunch.

She soon returned to the living room and placed a half sandwich and a glass of milk onto Ian's special table. He had just enough time to eat and brush his teeth before Nick was to drive him to his kindergarten class.

Alone in her large house, Dominique locked the doors and went to her new indoor pool to take a swim. She stripped to her birthday suit and set her foot on the top step. She descended slowly into the seventy degree water. After two laps, she adapted to the temperature.

Matt arrived home and with his key, he unlocked the house door. He entered and roamed the abode, searching for his wife. He heard soft splashing as he neared the annex. He stood in the entry and as he smoked a cigarette, he watched her.

Dominique caught sight of him and swam to her towel by the steps edge. "Are you coming in?" She enticed with her bare breasts, but knew he wouldn't because he was self-conscious about his patchy white legs.

He shook his head no.

She stepped out, wrapped the terry cloth around her, and joined Matt where he stood. "You're home early."

He leaned in and as he gently kissed her shoulder, he smelled the chlorine on her body. "They redid the schedule. I have to work the swing shift tomorrow." He pecked at her neck, causing her to giggle.

Just when Matt and Dominique exited from their bedroom, Nick and Wrek came home. They gathered in the kitchen where Wrek offered his sister, a sample dish of chicken fettuccine from his place of employment. "It's a new recipe."

She tasted it. "Mmm . . . You are such a good cook," she boasted, then took another bite before giving the pasta to Matt. She turned her attention to Nick. "How'd your GED class go?"

"Okay. They talked about punctuation today."

"Easy stuff. And I'm glad you've decided to further your education."

The telephone rang. Wrek who was the closest to an extension, answered it. He listened to the frantic caller on the other end. "Calm down," he told her, "I'll come see you." After he returned the receiver to the base, he looked at his sister with a sense of dread. "That was Nisa."

"I take it she's upset?"

"Yea. She received another letter. I'm going to go take a shower before I leave." He turned and walked away.

Dominique stood with her back against the counter. She drooped her head and gave thought to the situation and her money. "Maybe we should just go to the cops."

"We can't," Matt replied.

She slowly lifted her gaze to meet his. "Give me one good reason why we shouldn't."

"We can't prove it."

"What about the extortion notes?" she quickly added.

He paused. "We'd have to tell them about the mirror."

She sighed. "You're right. They wouldn't believe us." She rotated her position and looked out the window.

Matt stepped behind her and wrapped his muscular arms around her. "I'll go to Nisa's with Wrek and see what's going on."

A half hour later, Wrek and Matt went into the laundry room. Matt moved the mirror from the corner and shifted the glass about face while Wrek sat on the bench. "I want to smoke this before we go." He lit a joint.

Soon the two men stood before the arcane mirror. Wrek petted the mahogany frame, asking it to transport them to Phoenix; Matt for an hour, himself a few more. The reflector hummed a soft vibrant sound expressing its happiness as it gave off green sparks, then it took them through, one at a time.

Wrek landed next to his biblical fig tree while Matt appeared on the other side of the street. "I think this tree likes me," he spoke loudly to his brother-in-law as he crossed Sixth Street.

Nisa paced in her living room while she impatiently waited for Wrek. Having the jitters and sweaty palms, she smoked on a cigarette while she periodically glanced out the window. Her next peek, she observed Wrek and Matt nearing the edge of her yard. "Damn it. What's he doing here with Wrek?" She let the curtain fall back into place, then told herself to make it sound real. She opened the front door, hurried to Wrek, and embraced him as she broke down crying.

"Nisa, it can't be that bad," he spoke low as he enfolded his arms around and patted her back.

"Yes it is." She stepped back and wiped her tear. "Come in the house." She turned and led the two men into the kitchen where she revealed the letter.

Wrek opened it and read aloud. "Next time it will be YOUR heart I cut out. I want the rest of the money, forty eight thousand dollars." He looked at Matt with a wry face, then at Nisa. "What does this mean; Next time it will be YOUR heart I cut out?"

Nisa stepped aside, reached her hand into the sink and flipped the lid backwards from a cardboard box. "This was left on my porch this morning," she fabricated.

Wrek and Matt advanced and leaned in for a look. "Ew . . ." they both groaned when they saw a chunk of raw, bloody meat.

"It looks like a beef heart," Wrek commented, then poked at it with his finger.

Matt read the letter to himself as he fired up a cigarette. "It doesn't say when and where to take the money."

"I'll probably receive another letter in a day or so," Nisa proposed.

There was silence. Matt gave into heavy thought as he walked back and forth a few times across the kitchen floor.

"What are you thinking?" Wrek asked him.

He suspended his walk and peered at them. "A video camera," he spoke with a grin, "We set up a hidden video camera on her front porch and catch Paul delivering the note, then BAM!" He smacked his right fist onto his opposite palm. "We have more evidence and take it to the police."

Nisa was furious beneath her skin when she heard Matt's plan.

Wrek focused in on his girlfriend. "Sounds like maybe we can finally catch him."

She forced herself to smile.

Green fog became apparent in the corner of the room. "It hasn't been an hour," Matt remarked to Wrek. "I'll get the video equipment and come back through in a few hours." He walked toward and entered the cloudy mass where he was evaporated.

Nisa advanced to Wrek and wrapped her arms around him. "I'm scared. The thought of Paul coming to my house . . ." She lifted her head and cast her deceiving eyes upon his. "Why didn't your sister pay all of it the first time? Then we wouldn't even be in this darn mess."

"I didn't know they paid only two thousand until we were ransacking Paul's house."

Nisa kept quiet and veered from the tender subject.

"Do you want me to stay here with you for a few days?"

"I don't think my Aunt Penny would let you." As she withdrew her arms from him, she inhaled a whiff of his cologne. "Mmm . . . you smell good. You want a beer?"

"I want something alright," he expressed with a simper.

She stepped to the refrigerator, took two cans out of the bottom drawer, and handed one to her beau.

After opening their alcoholic beverages and taking a drink, they stood silent, staring and sending each other promiscuous looks.

She blew him a kiss.

He whispered, "I love you."

She was pleasantly surprised.

SIXTEEN

A SUGGESTION

MATT AND WREK returned home together by way of the mirror when they were done installing a micro camera within a plant that hung from Aunt Penny's porch.

Dinner was cooked and eaten. Nick and Travis loaded the dishwasher while Dominique wiped the counters and table.

"Mom. I need a new pair of drumsticks," Travis informed as he put the last of the plates into their slot. "One of mine broke today and the teacher let me borrow one of his."

"You're lucky I'm going into Coeur d' Alene tomorrow."

"I also need a new stand."

"Why?"

"The height adjustment lock is stripped."

She thought. "Well, you've had the drum since the fifth grade."

"Yea," Nick began to tease as he poured some detergent into the soap slot. "You've had it since you had to pull it to school in your little red wagon."

"That was sure embarrassing."

Dominique wanted to ease his self-image. "You were just too small of a kid to carry that large case."

Nathan entered the kitchen. "I called Sandy's mom."

Dominique gave him her undivided attention.

"He gets out December twenty third."

"At least he'll be home for Christmas."

"Can we buy him a nice gift?"

"Sure." She set the washcloth onto the sink's center. "Who wants to play water volleyball in a little while?"

The time was a quarter past seven when Dominique and her boys changed into their swimming suits and headed to their indoor pool. Matt and Wrek cracked themselves a beer as they went into the living room. After anchoring their tired bodies onto the couch, there was a knock on the door. They looked at each other. "You get it," they both spoke.

Matt groaned as he arose. He walked to and after opening the entry, his mood changed. "Hey Dash. Come on in."

Dash returned the greeting and stepped in carrying a bottle of vodka. He sat down on the matching blue love seat and secretly scanned the locality. "Where's your family?" he asked, aching to know where Dominique was.

"They're in the pool."

He took a swig of his liquor. "So why aren't you two swimming?"

"I don't swim," Matt stated.

"We're just relaxing after a long day," Wrek added.

"They're keeping you busy at work or what?" he asked Matt.

"That too. We've got the big bosses coming in from Boise so I have to work the swing shift tomorrow."

"That's a bummer," he spoke, but didn't share his sentiment, then he changed the subject. "I've been tinkering with a motorcycle I bought from my neighbor."

"Oh yea," Matt was intrigued. "What make?"

"A seventy-nine Yamaha."

Soon the three men were smoking pot and feeling tipsy. Dash cast his eyes upon Wrek. "So where's your girlfriend?"

"Where's yours?"

"Don't have one."

"Nisa's at home."

"Having love troubles?" he jested.

"No—nothing like that. She's just safely there right now." Wrek continued talking. "She's being threatened by . . ." He casually explained that someone wanted money from her, and Dominique agreed to pay the ransom.

Dash's face exploded with interest. "You should be there with her."

"I tried, she said her Aunt Penny wouldn't like it."

"How much is this person or persons asking for?"

"Another forty-eight thousand."

Nick entered the living room with a towel wrapped around him. He overheard Wrek and Matt's loose lips as they talked of the extortion letters. He stepped forward. "Hey Dash. When did you get here?"

"A while ago. Are you done swimming?"

"Yea. I'll be back." He turned and scampered up the stairs to his bedroom.

Dash returned his attention to the money. "Do you know who's blackmailing her?"

"We think it's her ex-boyfriend Paul," Matt disclosed.

"You know where this guy lives?"

"Phoenix."

"Arizona?" He offered up a strange look. "And where does Nisa live?"

"Phoenix."

"I'm confused," he chuckled as he swayed his head, then looked at Wrek. "How did you get involved with someone in Phoenix, if I may ask."

Silence filled the room.

"Well . . ." Matt began to say, "You're not going to believe this . . ."

Dominique and Ian walked in on the guy's conversation. "Matt?" she vocalized quickly. "Come here please."

He followed her to their bedroom and closed the door.

"Don't tell him about the mirror," she whispered.

"He won't say anything."

"Don't be so anxious to trust him, my love."

When Matt resurfaced into the living room, Wrek was telling his buddy about the first drop. He lit a cigarette and claimed his spot on the couch.

Dash also lit a tobacco stick as he observed Matt with wonder. "What are you going to do about Paul?"

"Since our first plan didn't work, we'll just hand over the money."

"Just out of curiosity, why haven't you got the cops involved?"

Matt raised a brow and peered at Dash. "Do you like cops?"

"I see your point." This was good news to his inner self. "But if you just hand over the money," he quoted while he used his index and middle fingers as bunny ears, "Who's to say he won't ask for more?"

Wrek shrugged his shoulders.

"You have to get rid of this guy," Dash stressed.

"What do you suggest?"

Wrek's ears were wide open.

Dash scanned the entryways and stair unit before he softly voiced his answer. "A bomb."

Matt leaned forward. "What?"

"Just a small one," he proposed. "I can make one explode when he opens the briefcase or a small box."

"No way!" He reclined into his seat while in heavy thought. "I told myself when I was released from prison that I would never do anything to return to that place."

"Okay," Dash surrendered, "I'll back off."

Wrek stood. "I'm going to go call Nisa," he spoke as he left the room.

Nick descended from his bedroom in black jeans and a gray sweat shirt. His wet hair was combed back and a soft down was visible above his lip. He walked toward the front door to exit, then turned. "Dash. You want to go for a cruise in my Charger?"

"Sure," he replied as he stood. "I'll see you later Matt."

While Nick led the way through the darkness toward the garage, he lit a cigarette.

"You smoke?"

"Yea, but don't tell my mom or Matt." He opened the motorized garage door before climbing into his orange car. He stuck the key into the ignition and after sparking the system, he revved the engine. "Feel that power!" he exclaimed.

"Where we going?" Dash who was feeling a buzz, slurred from the passenger seat.

"I want to drive by a girl's house." He switched on the heater.

"Mmm. The wanting of a woman. There is a certain fine woman I want and she lives in that house we just left," he spoke as he pointed.

"My mom?" He looked at Dash.

Not considering Nick's age, he said, "I could bend her over and love on her all night."

"Oh Dude, that's gross!"

Dash's intoxicating breath filled the air in the car causing Nick to crack his window. He turned on the headlights and backed out.

It had only been fifteen minutes from the time Nick and Dash left to the moment they returned to the estate. "I'd take you on a longer cruise, but my curfew tonight is ten o'clock."

"That's okay."

Nick took hold of the remote control from the dashboard and pushed the button. The automatic door on the garage lifted, then he drove in.

Matt had gone to bed and the boys were in their bedrooms. The living room light was dim and Dominique was lying on the recliner watching television. She was arrayed comfortably in sweat pants and a soft airy shirt.

"Come on in," Nick spoke to Dash, "I'll run upstairs and look for that issue."

Dash closed the door and strolled toward Dominique. "Hey Good-Looking. Nick's just grabbing a motorcycle magazine for me to borrow."

"Hmm." She toked on a joint then handed it to him.

He took a hit and when he passed it back to her, he let it drop onto her puss. "Whoops. Sorry," he remarked with a smirk.

She quickly grabbed the marijuana cigarette before it burnt through her clothing or rolled down in between her legs. "Sure you're sorry," she teased.

Wrek entered the room, anxious to speak. He first sniffed the air. "Mmm, I smell pot." He sat on the love seat. "I just got off the phone with Nisa," he told his sister. "She received a phone call from the blackmailer."

Dominique set the recliner upright and continued to listen.

"He said to have the money ready in a briefcase."

When Dash heard this, a bell sounded within his head.

"He said to wait two days and he'd get a hold of her again for the time and location." He paused to toke. "No cops . . ."

"Was it Paul's voice?" she asked.

"She said it was muffled."

There was silence.

"He must be watching her house. He has to know about the hidden camera," Wrek stated, "That is why he called instead of send another note."

Dominique cleared her throat. "This whole thing is starting to annoy me," she said firmly.

"You still have that black briefcase?" Wrek asked her.

She nodded and spoke low. "I'll go to the bank tomorrow."

Nick hurried down the steps with the magazine in hand. He stepped and relinquished the periodical to Dash. Everyone was eyeing Nick's guest, expecting him to arise and leave.

Dominique yawned.

He took the hint. As he left, he ached to hear more of their intriguing words, but didn't want to appear nosy. After he closed the entry, he stood idle and touched his ear onto the door. He heard nothing. He lit a cigarette and soon the porch light went off. He became aware of the turning doorknob, so he hopped aside and watched the door open to a crack.

"Are you going to go see Nisa tomorrow?" Dominique asked her brother, then blew her cigarette smoke out the open space.

In Phoenix? Dash pondered as he gave ear.

"Yea," Wrek replied. "She wants me to go play bingo with her cuz her Aunt Penny will be out of town." There was silence while he inhaled, then exhaled. "I'll be getting some muff too."

"Now that's nasty," she remarked.

Wrek grinned through the dark room even though she couldn't see. "Nasty for you, but lucky for me. I'm also lucky to have that awesome mirror to transport me to different places."

Dash was elated. His eyebrows went up and his mouth fell open.

SEVENTEEN

A VIOLATION

THE SUN WASN'T up yet when Aunt Penny arose from her bed and walked into the kitchen to start the coffee. While it brewed, she returned to her bedroom and dressed. She then carried her purse and a small suitcase to the living room where she placed them by the front door. When she went into the kitchen, Nisa was pouring a cup of the hot liquid. "Good morning," she greeted her niece.

"Morning Auntie. I see you're all ready to go." Nisa wore an ivory colored bathrobe, and her brown moccasins defined her native heritage.

"Just about, I have to drink a cup of coffee while I apply make-up to my face," she replied as she reached for a cup. "I left my car keys on my nightstand for you. Good luck winning at bingo tonight."

"Yea, maybe I'll win the jackpot." She would miss her aunt who is going to be away for the next three days at a conference in Las Vegas. Nisa sauntered into the dim living room while she enfolded her hands around the cup and sipped her tonic beverage. She sat on the couch and placed her feet at the edge of the coffee table.

After a few minutes, Penny finished brushing her auburn hair and took her last intake of coffee before setting the cup in the sink. She advanced to the front room. "The taxi should be here soon." She approached Nisa, bent down and kissed the top of her head.

"I know," Nisa remarked because of the affection, "I was my mother's papoose."

Penny gave thought to her own sister Tilly, who at a young age of sixteen, gave birth to two babies; the boy subdued from existence. She recalled her sister's glowing smile from the hospital bed as she held her new little girl. However, since Tilly's sudden death fourteen years ago, she felt obligated, yet honored to care and parent her niece. "You be good while I'm gone." She winked, then opened the door to leave.

Dominique yawned as she braked for a stop sign. She and Matt were strapped into their seat belts just as Ian was fastened into his booster seat. They were driving away from the high school after dropping Travis off for the day. She accelerated forward, then turned right onto a ramp and entered the freeway. The trio headed to the city.

In Coeur d' Alene, Dominique drove her car onto the bank's blacktop and parked in a space. "Let's hope they don't ask too many questions," she spoke to Matt as she lifted the latch and opened the door.

"It's your money. They shouldn't say shit about it," he replied.

"Yea, but forty-eight thousand is quite a withdrawal." The cool breeze caught her long hair when she stood. She zipped her jacket as she waited for Ian to step out of the car.

It took a short time for the bank teller to collect and count out the money.

As Dominique accepted the much cash, she ached from her gut, knowing that her money was going to pay off a blackmailer so her brother's girlfriend will be safe. "What a good sister I am or maybe, I'm just being stupid?" she spoke with sarcasm to Matt while they exited the building.

"You're not being stupid. You just care." He lit a cigarette. "I'm glad you had the extra money to help."

"You know," she talked while they went to the car. "After all this is over, I think Wrek needs to move out of our house and move in with Nisa like he told me he was going to. Then we need to do something about that mirror."

"The mirror ain't bad." Matt opened the driver's side door and sat. He drove his wife and stepson to the music store on Government Way where she purchased a new snare drum stand for Travis.

Inside the establishment, Ian was awed by the shiny displays of drums, cymbals, and guitars.

Matt then cruised the few blocks to the mall. A mild rainfall was mixed within the wind, blowing against their faces as they rushed to the entrance doors. Dominique held onto Ian's hand.

"Why are we here Mommy?"

"There's an awesome shirt on sale that I want to buy."

As they walked through the large walkway, Dominique window shopped a few businesses before entering their designated store. Once inside, Matt headed to the tool section while Dominique took Ian up the escalator to the women's department where she quickly searched and found the right size and color blouse.

She peeked at her watch. She knew, even after a quick lunch, that Ian would be late for his kindergarten class. She paid for her garment, then returned to the entrance door and out the entry where she and Ian sat on a bench and waited for Matt.

They weren't sitting long when Dominique recognized, within the crowd, a familiar face nearing.

"There's Dash Mommy!"

He approached them. "Hey . . . It's my favorite author lady," he spoke in a winsome manner. "Where's Matt?"

"He's still browsing." While they chatted, Ian leaned forward and peeked into his shopping bag to see his purchase.

Dash cleverly pulled the paper receptacle to his leg, letting the top close to conceal what was inside. He then left suddenly.

Ian watched him walk away. "Mommy?" He looked up at her. "Did my daddy look like him?"

"You know what your dad looks like. You've seen pictures."

"Not for a while," he replied.

"Well you can look at the photo albums this evening after school."

Ian was always interested in talking about his dad, learning and remembering what he could. "How did my daddy die?"

"In a truck accident. I told you that." She didn't want her five year old to know that Andrew was really blown to kingdom come when a bomb exploded in his truck. "Here comes Matt. Let's go." They stood to leave.

After returning to Kellogg, Dominique let Ian off at school and delivered the drum implement to Travis.

Once home, inside her bedroom, she slipped her shoes off and set her purchases onto the bed. She turned to Matt who was removing his cowboy boots and western shirt. She stepped behind him, wrapped her slender arms around his waist, and as she pressed her breasts against his back, she smelled his manly scent upon his white t-shirt. "Take me big man," she spoke in a whisper.

He giggled. It was nice to feel her warm body, but he didn't have time. "I have to leave for work in ten minutes."

"Ohh . . . ," she moaned with disappointment, then let go of him.

He pivoted. "It'll have to wait until I get home tonight." They kissed.

Wrek emerged through the mirror with seductive thoughts on his mind. He walked the Sixth Street sidewalk and soon came upon Nisa's place of residence. He stopped and eyed the rose bush. He hadn't picked a flower for his minikin in a while so he readied his pocket knife and cut the stem of a red rose. He went to her door, knocked, and waited.

The wooden structure opened and Nisa stood alone in a thin pink shirt and black panties. She held a beer and a smile.

"Mmm . . . I like what you're wearing," he spoke as he studied her hard nipples.

"I've been waiting for you."

He stepped in and closed the door.

She took him by his hand and led him to her bedroom. She stopped beside the bed and turned herself about.

"You're going to get it now woman!" He pressed his lips onto hers as he wrapped his arms around her waist and adjusted his hands onto her ass.

Matt was at work and Nick was still away visiting a friend. Dominique was in the kitchen preparing dinner for just herself and three of her sons.

"Boys! Ian," she called for as she stepped into the living room. "It's time for dinner." Ian had the photo albums scattered about the carpeted floor.

Travis and Nathan came rushing down the staircase.

"What are you two doing up there?" she asked when she saw their red faces and sweaty hair.

"Just our wrestling." They had taken their mattresses off from the frames and placed them up against the walls and shelves.

"So who's winning?" She showed interest while they walked into the dining room.

"It's a tie right now," Travis answered as he panted.

Ian sat into his chair. "Mmm," he exclaimed, "Hamburgers and flench flies."

While Nisa obtained a head start in the shower, Wrek who was nude, went to the kitchen for a beer. He cracked one open and as he took a drink, he saw a fashion magazine atop of the counter. He returned his cigarette to his lips and puffed as he set his can on a washcloth and opened the circular to page one. While he skimmed through it, a cut-up page caught his attention, then he closed up the magazine. He grabbed his beer and while he smoked on his tobacco stick, he directed himself down the hall toward the bathroom.

After the shower, they dressed. Nisa wore her moccasins and jeans with her carmine blouse. Her thick black hair was neatly brushed into a clip and her new ruby earrings sparkled red. She was in a cheery mood as they headed into the kitchen. She whistled a tune before speaking. "Are you still going to the bingo hall with me?"

"Sure," he replied, but his mind was focused on something else. He stepped to the counter where the magazine lay and after opening it to the cleaved page, he asked her about it.

There was worry within her heart, but she managed an answer. "A coupon," she spoke, "I cut out a coupon. What of it?" She stepped to the counter, took hold of the periodical, and tossed it into the garbage can. "Are we going to review those surveillance tapes before bingo or what?"

Wrek was relieved when she claimed it was a coupon. He just smiled and followed her into the living room.

The boys were done with their showers and ready for bed. Ian wore his rugrats pajamas while Travis and Nathan donned shorts and t-shirts. They were in the living room relaxing and watching TV.

Nick came home and went straight to the refrigerator for some eats.

Dominique joined him in the kitchen for conversation.

A knock at the front door interrupted the movie. Travis arose and answered it. He sent Dash to the kitchen.

"Hey guys!" Dash greeted as he stepped into the room, hoping for a friendly welcome.

After a hello, Dominique cocked an eye at the clock and knew it was kind of late for him to be visiting, especially with Wrek in Phoenix and Matt at work.

"What time does Matt get home?" Dash inquired.

"Eleven-forty, about an hour from now," she replied.

The trio stepped out onto the back porch for a joint. Dominique sat on her wooden swing beside Nick who was trying to quickly finish his sandwich.

The lighting was dim. Dash stood on Dominique's side of the swing. His genital bulge was within viewing range of her eyes. She tried not to peek, but her sinful desire let her take glances.

When the boys' movie was over, Dominique excused herself for a bit. She sent the three younger boys to bed, then went around saying her good nights to them, starting with Ian.

Nick and Dash parked themselves on the couch and watched a sports channel. Soon Nick arose and started for the bathroom. The telephone rang. "Get that!" he asked his guest.

Dash swiftly lifted the receiver. He politely informed the caller that he thought Dominique was in bed and he'd take a message for her.

Matt didn't want to disturb his wife's sleep so he trusted his friend to leave her a note to let her know he had to work the graveyard shift for a second night.

Dash set the receiver onto the base and as he remained on the sofa, he began to have thoughts of Dominique, alone, in that large bed.

Nick stepped into the room and yawned. "Who was on the phone?"

"My sister. She wants me to stop by Conoco."

Nick yawned again.

Dash took the hint. "I should leave." While he arose and walked to the door, Nick picked up the remote and turned off the TV. Dash opened the door and whirled himself about. "You want this locked?" he asked.

"Yea," Nick answered as he offed the foyer light.

Dash simulated turning the lock, then he closed the door.

Nick walked to the stairwell. He used the strip of light from the staircase trim to guide his way up to his bedroom. He closed his door and succumbed to his own television and bed.

Dash went to his truck and sat within the cab while he waited for time to pass. He was parked away from the streetlight, facing the quarter moon, yet he had full frontal view of Dominique's house as well as Matt's parking spot.

Dominique had felt the sniffles coming on so she took a dose of cold medicine to help her sleep. After a quick bubble bath, she slipped into a nightgown, smoked a cigarette as she stood beside her slightly open bedroom window, then went to bed.

Dash attained his miniature flashlight and a black case then, without a sound, he left his vehicle. He ventured to the front door of the house. In his gut, he felt a bit nervous, but it was so much money and if nobody messed with the briefcase, Paul would be the only one to die and nothing could ever be traced back to him.

Dash inched the unlocked door open and stepped in. All was quiet. He was sly as he tiptoed across the carpeted floor towards Dominique's bedroom. He noted the blue night light that emitted into the hallway from the bathroom. He came upon her bedroom door and turned the knob. As he entered her dim room, he became aware that his dream was lying on her side, facing the wall. He shut and locked the door before using his flashlight to search for the other black briefcase. He advanced to the closet and scanned amongst the top shelf, then the flooring.

While he hoped Dominique wouldn't wake, he moved to check between the nightstand and bed frame of Matt's side, then hers. He went to his knees and elbows, then he aimed his light underneath the bed. It was there.

He set his wee flashlight on the floor and pulled the briefcase towards him. He clicked it open, lifted the top, and stared at the money. He soon closed the portable case and opened his.

He gently obtained the appropriate colored wire from the C-4 block and plugged the extremity of it into the detonator, then he assumed a different colored wire from the battery and connected it as well. He pressed a button on the detonator to activate the system, closed the lid, and pushed the bomb underneath the bed.

With thoughts of Dominique, he crawled back to Matt's side and arose to a sit on his knees. He stretched his arm across the bed and slightly lifted the blanket. With his other hand, he aimed the flashlight in for a peek. Fuckin' damn she's beautiful, he rejoiced within his mind.

He set the flashlight underneath the bed and took off his clothes. Fully erected, he climbed into the bed and lay close to her.

"Matt?" she moaned in her sleep.

"Shh . . ." he hushed as he placed his tense hand onto and caressed her hip.

"Mmm . . ."

He soon introduced his hand to the inside of her panties.

Dominique adjusted her leg for she wanted Matt to have easier access.

Dash pulled the bikini garment aside and scooted next to her. He started intercourse.

Some two minutes and Dominique was too weary and drugged when sex was done; she fell back to sleep.

Dash quickly dressed, gathered his flashlight and briefcase, and exited the bedroom.

Just as he closed the bedroom door, he saw green flashes coming from the next room, then the light came on. He stood idle in the hallway corner.

Wrek closed the laundry room door from the inside.

Dash exhaled a sigh of relief before stepping past the closed door. With a smile upon his face, he crept through the house, out the door to his truck, and away from the premises. "That was too easy!" he boasted to himself.

EIGHTEEN

THE EXPLOSION

Dominique awoke and remembered the quick and intense sex that came upon her just hours ago. After sitting, she lit a cigarette and noticed, because of the ruffled blankets, that Matt had already awoken and left the bedroom.

Through the dusky room, she stood and slipped on her shorts before heading out to the kitchen to see who was available. The smell of freshly brewed coffee from Wrek's coffeepot enhanced her cheery mood.

Matt and Wrek were at the table, eating toaster waffles and drinking coffee.

She moved briskly to the refrigerator where she grabbed her preferred beverage, a soda. She opened the bottle and took a drink before stepping to Matt. She patted him atop of his helmet hair. "Aren't those the same clothes you wore yesterday?" she asked him with an odd look.

"Yea, they are," he answered, "I just got home ten minutes ago. A co-worker didn't show up for work so I had to work a double shift." He took a bite of waffle. "Didn't Dash tell you that I called?" He cast his eyes upon her as he chewed.

That Bastard! She thought, realizing that she'd been sexually violated. She looked at her husband and spoke quietly, holding in the truth. "He did." Being in shock, she didn't quite know what to do. If she told Matt, he might blame her and want to leave, yet she didn't want to hurt his feelings. "I'm going to go take a shower." She left the room in a different frame of mind.

"I'll come join you in a bit," he remarked.

Matt and Wrek both glanced at the clock when the telephone rang.

"Who'd be calling at seven-thirty?" Wrek wondered as he arose from his chair. He then went to the communication device and lifted the receiver. "Talk to me."

"He just called!" Nisa blurted.

"Paul?"

"Yes Paul. His voice was disguised again, but I know it was him. He wants his cash today." She began to fuss.

"Don't worry my Minikin, we've got it under control."

"He said next time nobody will find me, that's why I'm so afraid."

"What time does he want the money?"

"Two o'clock. He also said to come alone."

"Where?" Wrek was now concerned.

"The exit-137 truck stop."

Matt overheard Wrek's replies as he finished eating. He then slipped his plate and fork into the dishwasher, walked to his bedroom, to the bathroom where he undressed and stepped into the shower. It was awesome, he thought, to have two overhead nozzles in one showerstall. He could watch the soap and water stream down his wife's naked body while he too showered. "You still want to do it?" he asked her.

She felt guilty. "You're probably too tired. We can wait," she told him.

He then yawned.

"See?" She turned the water off on her side, took hold of a towel, and stepped out.

Matt went to bed and fell asleep while Dominique drove Travis and Nathan to school. She came home and inserted a movie into the VCR for Ian before going to the kitchen to wipe counters and start the dishwasher.

Nick entered the kitchen.

Dominique observed him. "You're up early for a Friday."

He cracked a smile. "I'm thirsty." He opened the cupboard, grabbed a glass, then opened the refrigerator.

"What time did Dash go home last night?"

"Uh . . . about eleven thirty."

"Did you lock the front door after he left?"

"He locked it."

No he didn't, she thought. "New rule for everyone! No company after eight o'clock," she ordered, then left the room.

Ian was soon bored with his movie. He exited the living room and wandered through the hallway towards his mom's bedroom. He turned the knob and slowly pushed open the door. "Mom?" he whispered as he poked his head in. He heard the sound of the fan and saw that Matt was sleeping so he entered.

After Dominique left the kitchen and noticed a vacant living room, she searched for her missing child; first in his bedroom, then the bathroom.

Ian tiptoed to his mom's side of the bed and opened her nightstand drawer. He eyed some contents, then closed the wooden fitting. He laid on his stomach and as he peeked under the bed, he saw the black briefcase. He grabbed the handle and pulled it near. "This looks like Dash's," he spoke, then set his fingers onto the latches.

Jasmine sat on the carpeted floor in her living room. As the stereo played a soothing melody, she rummaged through the old trunk that Matt had taken down from Stanley's attic. She placed two infant moccasins within her hands and looked them over. "They're cute," she remarked, then wondered why her late husband had these odd itmes, for she knew he wasn't of the Native American pedigree.

She took hold of and studied a silver necklace, a small ceramic figure of a warrior, and a coiled wicker basket that contained three stone arrowheads and a few feathers. She unfolded and took a look at a handwoven blanket before she reared up a photograph. It was of a female papoose.

David carried into the living room, a box. Before he set it on the floor next to his mother, he blew a small amount of dust from atop of the cardboard. It caught his attention when green dots twinkled, then disappeared. He shook his head in disbelief. "Open this one carefully," he told his mom.

Jasmine gazed with wonder at the tarnished box, then drew the flaps back. She leaned forward just slightly, and viewed the miscellaneous items. She picked up a wooden tomahawk and in a playful manner, she chopped it onto the edge of the box.

David sat on the couch and watched.

She lifted a few envelopes from the eerie box and noticed they were old and yellow. She looked for the postage dates. "Oh wow," she spoke in a low tone. "Nineteen fifty-nine." She glanced at David. "This was only two years before I met your dad." She pulled the piece of paper into view and uncreased it. It was a handwritten letter that started with Dearest Stanley. She mumbled as she read. "Don't be angry with me. As you know I am only sixteen and I have no choice but to have these babies and give them up for adoption. My sister Penny says young girls don't have babies without being married, and if I tried to see you, she would file rape charges against you." Jasmine left thetip of her fingernail on the spot where she ended her reading, then realized her late husband's deception. "Oh my gosh! He had children with another woman."

"I guess that would explain why nobody was allowed up in his secret little attic," David spoke as he bunny eared.

Jasmine finished reading the letter. It was signed by Tilly.

There were a few more envelopes, one held a ring. She eyed the gem and knew it was probably a promise or engagement ring. She lowered her head and started weeping. "He never told me how serious he was about Tilly."

David arose from the sofa and fetched a box of tissues, then stepped to his mom. With compassion in his heart, he sat on the floor and embraced her with an arm. "He was always an insensitive worm."

She dabbed her eyes with the tissue, then reached into the box for a picture. She studied the photo; the photo of two Native American babies that were wrapped in the handwoven blanket she previously held. There were two names written on the picture's edge, but they were barely legible. "Mathew and Nisa. MATHEW?" She raised her eyebrows as she apprehended this new information. "I adopted Stanley's biological son and Stanley knew it all these years!" She cast her aching eyes to David. "Matt has a twin sister named Nisa."

Jasmine scanned the few remaining envelopes and came upon a copy of a birth certificate and legal papers from nineteen sixty that released the custody of the boy to the State.

One last old mailer was a letter that Stanley had written to Tilly, but was returned. Jasmine was too nervous, she had David read the message.

"He says to her that he is now married to you, says he hopes the baby is doing fine. He was glad to hear that Penny helped her to keep the girl after the boy died." David cast his attention to his mom's facial expression. "Tilly thinks Matt died at birth."

"Sounds like Penny was a handful, wouldn't let Stanley see Tilly or the baby. She and Stanley lied about the boy and I bet she forged Tilly's name on the adoption papers."

"Why would Stanley team up with Penny and lie about Matt?"

"God only knows," she replied.

A brown envelope was tucked under the bottom flap. Jasmine picked it up. It was dated April of seventy-four. She took hold of and unfolded the letter. She looked to see that it was sent by Penny who wrote of Tilly's sudden death.

Jasmine turned off her stereo and paced the floor in heavy thought. She told her younger son that she should soon tell Matt about his biological parents and his twin sister.

In her bedroom, Dominique crept up to Ian, knelt, and grabbed onto his wrist. "What are you doing?" she whispered.

Ian let go of the latches. "Nothing," he said in a frightened manner.

"Push that back under the bed."

Ian obeyed, then followed his mother out to the hall.

"You go sit on your bed until lunch," she scolded. "You know you're not suppose to sneak into my bedroom."

"Sorry Mom, I thought it was Da . . ."

Ian was interrupted by Wrek who approached them. "What's going on?"

Ian turned and drooped his head as he walked to his bedroom.

"I need to talk to you," Dominique spoke to her brother as she began the jaunt to the laundry room.

Wrek flipped on the exhaust fan and pulled a bag of weed from his jeans pocket before sitting on the stoner's bench next to Dominique. "Pour your heart out Dom," he said.

"It's not really pouring my heart out." She observed him loading his pipe. "Something happened and I'm too scared to tell Matt." She paused. "Last night Dash came into my bedroom."

Wrek looked at her with a raise of the eyebrows.

"I thought it was Matt. He climbed into bed and I don't remember anything except the sex."

"What?" He seemed shocked, but interested. "You have to tell Matt."

She let a tear drip. "I feel guilty because I enjoyed it."

"Well it's up to you if you want to tell him or not. I'll keep quiet about it." He toked on his pipe.

When Dominique went into Ian's bedroom, he was asleep on his bed. "Ohh . . . ," she moaned as she stepped to him. She bent down and kissed him on the forehead.

He opened his eyes.

"It's time to wake up for lunch and school."

"Do I have to go?" He turned over and closed his eyes.

She sat at the edge of his bed and took hold of his small delicate hand. She adored her five year old Baby Zebra. She gently pulled on his arm. "You have to go, it's art day and you have to finishing molding your elephant."

He stretched and sat up.

Dominique stood and lifted her son up into her arms. As she embraced him, she turned and carried him into the kitchen.

After Dominique drove Ian to school, she promptly returned home. Matt was awake when she and Wrek entered the bedroom. It was noon; time for Wrek to take the money through the mirror to Nisa's house.

"Be careful," Matt told him, "Just let her deliver the briefcase, then get her away from the truck stop."

Wrek left the bedroom feeling confident. He went to the laundry room and turned the mirror about face. He stood in front of it and lit a cigarette. As he puffed, he talked and caressed the mahogany frame. Soon the enchanted mirror pulled him and the briefcase through.

Wrek walked from his shade tree to Nisa's residence where he knocked on the door and waited.

Nisa opened the wooden entry.

"Hi my sweets," he spoke, then stepped in and kissed her. He looked into her mysterious green eyes. "What's the matter?"

"I'm just nervous, I guess."

"Don't be. I'm here with you." He held onto the briefcase while she gathered her wallet and keys.

In Aunt Penny's car, Nisa adjusted herself into the driver's seat while Wrek set the briefcase on the passenger's seat and climbed onto the back seat. He wanted to be hidden in case someone was watching and following her.

She reversed the auto out from the garage, down the driveway to the street, then accelerated forward.

Matt had just returned to sleep when Dominique entered the bedroom and sat at the rim of their bed. She woke him up with a rub to his hairy arm. "Your mom is here. She wants to talk to you."

"She never comes to visit me. It must be serious." He drew back the blankets and scooted out of bed. He lit a cigarette and while he dressed, Dominique watched.

In the living room, Matt listened to his mother speak of his biological parents and twin sister. She showed him the birth certificate and one of the letters. He was stunned. He felt overjoyed to have a sister, but was horrified to learn that Stanley, his mean-spirited adoptive father was also his natural father.

After Jasmine left, Matt turned to Dominique who was also in shock by this new information. "I have to go protect my sister." He was determined as he looked at his watch. "One fifteen. I still have time."

"Matt? What are you doing?" She expressed concern. "She's suppose to deliver the money alone."

He ignored her statement. "Give me all your cash."

She hurried to their bedroom where she emptied her wallet of bills, then returned to her husband. "All I have is a hundred and seven."

"That'll do." He took the wad and crammed it into his pants pocket. "Thank you." He stepped in and gently pulled her into his arms, then kissed her good bye. "Now I know why the mirror sent us to her." He went to the laundry room and closed the door. After talking and patting the frame, he was taken through.

Small bits of green gems twinkled from Matt's body into the air and evaporated as he headed for Nisa's house. He soon arrived and knocked on the door; he was hoping they hadn't left. When no one answered, he turned theknob, but it was locked. He cast his eyes to the left and then to his right, seeing if anyone was watching him.

Matt walked to the garage entrance. It was open so he stepped in and reclosed the door. He went to the second entry and tested the knob; it was locked. He lifted his leg and with his heel, he gave the door a kick. It swung open. He stepped into the kitchen where he used the telephone to call a cab.

Matt left Nisa's house and waited on the corner of Sixth Street. Some five minutes later, the taxi arrived, and he was on his way to the exit-137 truck stop.

Nisa drove into the smaller parking lot of the truck stop. The business was crowded, almost every parking space was taken. She circled the parcel of land before finding a spot between a van and compact car. "We're here," she told her obscured boyfriend.

Wrek sat up. "After you give him the money, drive back around and get me." He reached for the handle and opened the door two inches, then he looked again at Nisa. "I love you girl."

She looked back at him. "Likewise," she replied.

"Lovewise." He blew her a kiss, then stepped out onto the pavement and closed the door. He topped his head with a baseball cap and slipped on a pair of sunglasses. He walked towards the building.

Nisa backed the car out of the space and as she slowly cruised to the rear of the establishment, she glanced at the briefcase. She tapped it with her four fingers and smiled. "My money."

The cab driver let his passenger off at the front door of the truck stop.

Matt watched the taxi hasten away, then he scanned the area, searching for Wrek or Nisa. He walked up the sidewalk to the entrance, pulled the bar knob toward him, and entered the air conditioned mini store. He noticed the lines were long, people were buying snacks and paying for their fuel.

Nisa left the black top and drove on a dirt path toward the Dumpsters. Employee cars were lined in the center of the acre and a few vehicles were parked next to the building. She spied the area as she braked by one of the large Dumpsters.

Matt decided to return to the outdoors. He walked the sidewalk around the corner to the side of the building where he caught sight of Wrek.

Wrek was loitering about at the edge of the parking lot beside a light pole, smoking a cigarette. He was surprised to see Matt approach him. "What are you doing here?"

"You're gonna have a hard time believing this . . ." He briefed him on his mother's visit; her shocking information and the proof she bore.

Nisa took a handbag from under her seat, then grabbed the briefcase by the handle and exited her aunt's teal Ford. She stepped behind a metal garbage bin. "For my daughter, Rainy," she spoke to herself as she knelt, unfolded the handbag, and set her fingers onto the clasps. She clicked the fasteners open and lifted the lid. "BOOM!"

Wrek and Matt were stunned when the explosion sounded. They feared Nisa was involved as they hurried in the direction of the smoke. When they arrived at the scene, a hired security guard was standing close to a body, talking on his radio.

NINETEEN

A DOWNCAST DURATION

THE DAY HAD turned gloomy. Matt and Wrek paced the floor in the hospital's waiting room.

"I blame Paul," Wrek accused aloud. "He took the money and hurt my girl. Again." His speech quivered with anger.

Matt gave thought to the conversation he and Dash had last week. "It wasn't Paul's bomb." He stopped in the center of the room and set his focus on his brother-in-law.

Wrek drew his brows together. "What do you mean it wasn't Paul's?"

"Remember Dash's suggestion?"

He recalled it slightly. "Oh wow, you're right. That Bastard somehow switched briefcases." He thought of what Dominique had told him about Dash sneaking into her bedroom.

The doctor entered the lobby. "Nisa's family?" He cast his eyes about.

Matt stepped forward. "I'm her brother."

Wrek joined them.

"She's in very critical condition," he spoke with concern. "She might not make it through the night."

Wrek's face became pale. "Can we see her?"

"I would normally say no, but in this case, I will allow it. Wait here for the nurse." He turned and headed through the corridor.

Wrek went to a chair and sat. "My Minikin," he mumbled as he covered his face with his hands and wept.

Matt sat silently close to Wrek. He looked at the clock. The time seemed to be ticking slower than normal. His attention was diverted when two people entered the lobby.

The two strangers approached Matt and Wrek. "I'm Detective Laura Justice and this is my partner Steven Kribz." They presented their badges.

"What do you want with us?" Matt asked.

"You two were at the truck stop when the explosion happened?" Detective Kribz questioned as he raised an eyebrow.

Matt glanced at Wrek, then at the detectives. "Yea, I just found out she was my sister and I wanted to tell her."

"Why was she around back of the building?"

He felt confused within himself. How much information should he be giving out? he thought. "She said she was going to meet someone."

"Who?"

"There was a man blackmailing her. She had a briefcase full of money she was going to pay him."

The nurse walked into the room. "Who wanted to see Nisa?"

Matt and Wrek both arose from their seats and shifted their attention to the woman in white.

"Come with me," she instructed.

Detective Justice quickly reacted. "We'll be waiting. We still have questions for you."

"That's all I know," Matt replied as he exited the lobby with Wrek.

The two downcast men had to wash their hands and then attire themselves into sterile gowns and guaze masks.

"I don't know if I can handle seeing her all bandaged up," Wrek's voice trembled through his medical veil.

"I feel sick in my gut too," Matt consoled. "My sister's in a coma."

They followed the nurse's aide into the intensive care unit. Wrek felt his legs wobble as he neared the bed. He sat in the one chair, then slipped his hand under Nisa's precious hand. He swallowed to coat his dry throat, then he leaned in. "Hi Baby. It's Wrek," he whispered, "I'm here with you." Within a few moments, he felt her gently squeeze his hand. He choked down the lump in his throat. "I know you can hear me Nisa."

Matt stood beside Wrek and beheld her condition. He wanted to vomit, but held back. As he began to blame Dash again, his shaken nerves were turned to anger.

They were only allowed to stay but a minute.

"We're gonna get this guy who hurt you Nisa," Matt told his sister, but didn't tell her she was.

They left the patient area and disposed of the gowns and masks.

"I don't want to talk to those investigators right now," Matt expressed as he peeked around the corner.

The two absconders walked away from the lobby through the corridor towards another hallway where they called for the elevator. After they stepped into an empty transport, green fog appeared and floated within the air. They faded out and were pulled through to home.

Travis and Ian were standing by the laundry room door playing with their yo-yo's when Matt and Wrek came into being.

"Mom? Matt's home," Ian called to Dominique.

Dominique hurried to Matt who had went into their bedroom. "Are you okay?" she asked, then advanced forward and wrapped her arms around his waist to show that she too, was ill about Nisa. "What are her chances?"

"Not good."

She let go of his midsection and sat onto her antique sofa as she listened to him speak briefly of Dash.

Matt lit a cigarette. "I'm in a daze," he told her. "It doesn't seem real."

"I know the feeling. I was numb when Andrew died."

"Well, Nisa's alive, thank God!" He rarely spoke of the Lord, yet he knew he needed to pray more than what he did.

There was a moment of silence.

"Dinner's done. I made fried chicken."

"Sounds good, but I'll eat later. Wrek and I are gonna go take a ride out to Dash's place." He visited the restroom before leaving.

After Matt and Wrek left in the truck, Dominique gathered her sons for dinner. At the table, she informed them that Wrek's girlfriend Nisa, is Matt's twin sister. She also told them that someone was extorting money and Nisa was meeting the blackmailer today to pay him off when the exlosion occurred.

"Where was the bomb at?" Nick who already knew part of her story, asked as he buttered his roll.

Dominique took a portion of cranberry sauce and set it on her plate. "We think it was in a briefcase." She now wanted to limit her acquired facts.

Ian's eyes widened. "Dash's bwefcase?" he asked with a mouthful of potatoes.

She gave thought to her son's question. The image of him trying to open the briefcase popped into her mind. Could that of been the bomb? She cast her eyes upon Ian. "Did you see Dash go into my bedroom?"

"No Mama. I just saw his bwefcase in his chopping bag at the store."

Retribution surged through her body. She wanted that suave and charming criminal to pay for what he had done.

Matt exited the freeway and drove upon the streets of Smelterville. He turned into an alley and sped to the forth house. He braked and cut the engine before stepping out onto the gravel lane. He and Wrek spied the property as they walked through a gateway and around a small trailer. No one was around. It was quiet when they knocked on the trailer door: they knocked again.

"He's not home."

"That's because he has our forty-eight grand," Matt quickly vented. "He's living it up somewhere." He soon lit a cigarette, then turned and directed himself back towards his truck.

"What are we going to do?" Wrek asked as he followed.

"Go home and get drunk."

After stopping over at the bar for a beer on tap and a twelve pack, Matt drove home.

Dominique was just finishing the dinner dishes when her husband and brother returned home. "Did you find him?"

"He wasn't home," he replied as he carried his half case of beer to the refrigerator.

"So . . . now you're going to get drunk?"

"I get drunk every weekend. It's no big deal."

She knew it was useless to argue with someone who had been drinking. She learned that from her first husband. "If you think it will help," she mumbled as she walked out of the kitchen.

Wrek managed a few bites from a chicken breast before freshening himself in the bathroom. He mentioned to his sister that he was leaving to go see Nisa, then he continued on to the laundry room, closed the door, and sat upon the stoner's bench. He lit a joint and sat quiet as he inhaled and exhaled five hits. He stood to his feet and asked the mirror to send him to the hospital in Phoenix for two hours. He dabbed his marijuana cigarette into the ashtray seconds before green smoke was visible and the docile mirror exerted its force and drew him in.

Wrek landed in the men's lavatory on the second floor. Feeling paranoid from his high, he stepped lightly out of the privy and into the corridor. He peeked about for those detectives; he didn't see them. He journeyed up the hallway until he came upon the Intensive Care Unit. His heart was thumping. He wanted to see his woman even though she was painfully wrapped up in body gauze. He advanced to and looked through the window at the critical patients.

A nurse approached him. "Who are you looking for?"

He cast his eyes upon her caring face. "Nisa Waubay," he replied.

The nurse's expression changed. "Oh . . . the doctor was looking for you."

Wrek followed the attendant to the nurse's station where he waited for the physician.

Soon Doctor Fobbs advanced Wrek and informed him of Nisa's death. In a few words, he explained that her internal injuries and loss of body fluid put her into shock, thus stopping her heart.

Wrek turned aside. Hushed tears rolled down his cheek. "Oh Nisa." His gut ached. He felt paralyzed as he stepped away with wobbly legs. He walked unsteadily toward the elevator, but entered the stairwell.

Alone in the stairwell, he reclined against the wall and slid down onto a step. He bent forward until his midriff almost reached his friend's lap, then he placed his arms about his head onto his knees, and sobbed.

Matt was in the garage attempting to twist a screw from its hole on a broken portable heater. Soon he removed all the screws and metal cover. As he studied the interior components, he took drinks from his beer. He gave thought to yesteryear when he was a young teenager and the heater in his basement bedroom quit working. He had asked and hinted to his father to fix it, but Stanley was full of unjust excuses: You shouldn't of cranked and left it on high all day while you were at school. It's March, it ain't that cold.

Later in life, he learned that his father purposely took the element out so he could claim it was broken. A tear dripped from his eye. Why had his father been so spiteful to him? Had he known he adopted his own blood son? Matt's thinking shifted to his injured sister. He had always wanted to know where he came from and now that he knows, it could all be taken away.

Wrek was grieving when he left the hospital. He took a taxicab to Sixth Street, then paid the driver. Teary eyed, he approached Aunt Penny's house, walked the sidewalk to the garage door, and entered. He stood in the empty space where Aunt Penny's car should be parked and cast his eyes toward the slightly open door that Matt had kicked in.

He pushed in the broken door and entered the house. Within the kitchen he recalled memories of Nisa. Remembering how she stood so petite in front of the hot stove, preparing an old family recipe dinner of ham and honey flavored beans; how they sat amidst the candlelight drinking cherry wine and fornicating.

Wrek's gut continued to ache as he stepped into Nisa's bedroom. He stopped in the center of the room and cast his vision to her precious doodads and ceramic objects amongst her shelves and dresser. He then sat down on her purple bedspread at the edge of her bed and lit a cigarette. As he puffed, he scanned the walls, catching sight of her daughter's picture. "Oh . . . Rainy, Baby Girl."

After filling her bedroom with smoke, Wrek doused his cigarette into her ashtray. He extracted the drawer from her nightstand and snooped. He took hold of a small paperback book and read the cover. "How to Blackmail and Get Away With It." He brought his head up in thought. "Could she be?" He went to return the book to its place, then snagged it up again and closed the wooden unit. As he stuffed the book into his back pocket, he saw movement of green within the room and knew his time was up. "Please mirror," he spoke, "Take me to Dominique's back yard."

Wrek stood alone on his sister's property. Raindrops were falling from the dark sky so he hastened to the patio. He felt hesitant to step inside the house so he decided to ponder and wait a minute or two. His insides hurt; he knew he had to tell Matt and Dominique the bad news.

He soon entered through the rear door of the house and searched for his sister or brother-in-law. He located Matt exiting from the bathroom. He approached him. His lips wavered a few times, then he spoke with a dry throat. "Oh my God Dude, she died." He turned away; he didn't want Matt to see him cry.

Matt's face grew blank.

"Aunt Penny is going to freak," Wrek sobbed.

"I'm going to freak!" Matt roared, "At Dash!" He walked away from Wrek towards the kitchen where he grabbed four beers from the refrigerator. He exited through the rear door and returned to the garage.

After hearing voices through the thin cracks of her bedroom door, Dominique arose from her antique sofa and walked toward the exit. She opened the wooden closure and as she stepped into the hallway, she beheld Wrek's agony. She then pursued Matt.

Dominique heard the outside door close as she entered the living room. She turned off the kitchen's electrical sun and advanced outside with her jacket and umbrella. She saw the garage light emitting through the three inch space between the frame and door. She crept to the entry and when she became aware of Matt throwing a beer against the wall, she halted at the building's edge and spied through the gap.

Matt threw a second can, then a third; both bursting open and spraying liquid upon the walls and floor, all the while cursing aloud and ranting threats directed at his old cellmate.

Dominique felt somewhat afraid. She had never seen her husband this upset. Normally a teddy bear, he was now an angry grizzly.

"You will not get away with this Dash!" He seized the small portable heater that he'd been working on and heaved it against the wall. "I will find you even if it's the last thing I do!"

"Oh wow," she spoke under her breath as she watched broken pieces scatter onto the floor. She sensed that this would not be a good time to tell him what Dash had done to her.

TWENTY

WHERE'S DASH?

THE NEXT MORNING, Matt awoke needing aspirin. He stood by the kitchen window and swallowed five pills with a morning Pepsi, then he settled into a chair at the table with the newspaper and a cigarette.

Dominique joined her husband, adding a loaded bowl. She took a hit and as she passed the pipe, she eyed him. "I saw you last night . . . in the garage."

"Oh yea?" He kept his vision on the newspaper.

"You have a mess to clean up, huh?"

"I guess so." After a moment, he folded and set his read on the table top.

Dominique reached out and with her hand, she took hold of his grip and gently held on. There was stillness as she displayed affection for his loss. "What are you going to do?"

"I'm gonna go find Dash."

Her heart now panged at the say of that lawbreaker's name while Matt continued to disclose to her of Dash's suggestion. "He told me he could make one explode from a briefcase when it's opened."

Her eyes widened. "So it's true, Ian was right."

"Two nights ago when I worked that double shift, Dash answered the phone. Where were you?"

She let go of his hand and drew her arms to herself. "I went to bed early. I thought Wrek would see him out."

"He had to of snuck into our bedroom and snoop for the briefcase."

She knew he did. She lit a cigarette to help calm her nerves. "He was in the bedroom."

Matt's ears perked up. "How do you know?"

She was trembling, but she wanted to come clean, to keep no secrets from him. "I thought it was you." She hesitated. "He climbed into our bed and . . . fucked me."

"Oh my God!" His expression turned to anger.

"I'm sorry," she pleaded, "I didn't want to hurt your feelings."

His jaw hardened. He took in a deep breath and exhaled it. "Was he any good?"

"I thought it was you," she repeated, trying to be sincere, yet convincing. "I was out cold from medication."

With the back of his hand, Matt smacked his bottle of pop, knocking it across the table to the floor, then he stood to his feet.

Dominique was awed by his move, yet she could feel his pain.

"I'm going for a ride." He walked off.

Outdoors, the sun was hidden by cloud cover. Matt zipped his jacket as he went to and climbed into his truck. He started the engine, switched the heater on, and watched the windshield wiper's swipe the raindrops across the glass while his truck warmed.

Flashes of lightning brightened the gray sky as he drove to Smelterville. He steered into the alley and advanced to Dash's abode. He parked his vehicle and stepped around the small trailer to the front door. It was raining slightly as he knocked and scanned the neighborhood.

After he rapped again on the door, he stepped to the window and peeked in. The blue curtains were pulled back.

He could see the empty shelves, the bare section on the wall where a few pictures had hung, and his TV and VCR were missing from the stand. "That rat!" He turned away and returned to his truck.

Matt drove further down the road to his mom's residence, but didn't stop or go inside the house; her car was absent from its spot. He then cruised back to and within Kellogg before going home.

For the rest of the day, Matt moped. He stayed alone in his bedroom, sat on the bed, and watched television while he smoked weed.

Wrek did the same as Matt, except he cried in segments for Nisa.

Sunday came and gone. Monday morning brought in the sunshine once again. Dominique drove Travis and Nathan to school, then returned home.

After a few hours of cleaning and washing the laundry, she entered her bedroom and approached her reclusive husband who was lying in bed, smoking a cigarette. "Are you going to get up today?"

"Maybe," he spoke low.

She joined him on the bed and lit a cigarette as well. "I thought you were going after Dash?"

"I went to his trailer. He's gone."

"Yea . . . You do have a magic mirror, remember?"

Matt laid quiet as he gave thought to her idea and how he could actually capture him.

Inside the Public Safety Building, Detectives Laura Justice and Steven Kribz were reviewing the video tape from the truck stop. Laura, who was specialized in criminal profiling, wanted to take a closer look at Nisa Waubay's life. They played the surveillance tape from the parking lots, frame by frame. They saw Nisa exiting her car and while she walked toward a garbage bin, she carried the briefcase and handbag that were confiscated as evidence. "She's alone. I bet she was going to take the money from the briefcase and put it into that handbag," Detective Justice commented as she watched Nisa disappear behind the Dumpster.

"But there was no money," Steven replied.

"She didn't know that." She recalled what Matt had told them about Nisa going to meet and pay off the blackmailer. "Someone else took the money."

"And put the bomb in the briefcase."

"I think we need to go visit some people, find out who Nisa's brother is."

The detectives ran the license plate of the teal Ford through their system, then gathered their notebooks and cruised to Sixth Street.

Detective Justice knocked at the door and while she and Steven waited for a response, she looked about the porch and with a trained eye, she noticed a hidden camera.

The door opened and a plump woman with a sad countenance greeted them.

Laura introduced herself and Detective Kribz to Penny. "We are ached at the loss of your niece and very committed to solving this case," she spoke boldly, but with compasssion. "Can we come in?"

Aunt Penny stepped back and let them enter into her lifeless living room where they all sat down.

"Please Penny, tell us about Nisa."

Penny tried to keep from sobbing. "She was a beautiful young squaw and she left behind a thirteen year old papoose who I'm trying to gain visitation rights to." She choked on her words.

There was silence in the room. Laura observed the used facial paper and box of tissues on the coffee table as she opened her notebook. "What do you know about her blackmailer?"

"I don't know about any blackmailer. I do know that a few months ago, she was kidnapped and that's how she met her boyfriend, Wrek."

Laura removed from her notebook and showed her, a photo of the two men from the surveillance video. "Is one of these Wrek?"

Penny reviewed the picture. "Yes," she replied as she pointed to him.

"Do you know the other guy?"

"No."

"And where does this Wrek live?"

"Idaho. Northern Idaho," Penny claimed.

Laura emitted a strange look. "So they had a long distance relationship?"

"I guess so. He just showed up, but never drove an automobile."

Detective Justice asked, "Do you know where your niece got this so-called money?"

"No."

"And lastly, do you know who kidnapped her?"

"A man named Paul. Nisa didn't report it to the authorities. She told me she just wanted to forget about Paul and what he did to her so I didn't pressure her too much."

"That's fine," Laura consoled, then looked at Steven.

Detective Kribz leaned forward a bit. "We talked to someone who claimed to be Nisa's brother."

"She doesn't have a brother." Penny's mind wandered to yesteryear. Could it be? she thought, could Mathew be looking for his family roots? Maybe he's the other guy in the picture? She cast her eyes upon Detective Kribz and revealed to them of Tilly and Stanley's secret love affair and how it came to Stanley signing the boy twin up for adoption.

Soon enough, the detectives were searching through Nisa's dresser drawers and closet. They found nothing that would offer a clue. On their way out, they took a look at the broken kitchen door. "Paul?" Steven spoke as he glanced at Detective Justice.

Penny heard his question. "It happened while I was away."

"Is anything missing?"

"No, just my car," she clowned in spite of her tragedy.

"You'll get your car back from the lab in a day or two."

The detectives exited Penny's house and advanced to their state issued car.

"It sounds like we want this Paul guy, but first," Laura suggested to her co-worker as she opened the driver's door, "I think we might find out more if we fly to Idaho and question Wrek."

"If we find Wrek," Steven added, "We find Nisa's brother."

"Exactly. And then we can learn why they fled the hospital."

TWENTY ONE

NABBING DASH

MATT AROSE OUT of bed, showered and dressed. He went to the kitchen where Wrek and Nick were eating cereal. He sat in a chair and cast his attention on Wrek. "I have an idea. You want to go with me and capture that murderer?"

"I want to go!" Nick quickly volunteered. "My knee is feeling better."

Matt looked at him. "Maybe. Go ask you mother."

While Nick begged his mom for the bounty hunting experience, Matt and Wrek talked.

"I figure we'll ask the mirror to take us to where Dash is, handcuff him, then bring him through the mirror to Arizona."

Matt kissed his wife good bye with a quick peck, then she left the laundry room and closed the door.

The three eager pursuers stood in front of the large mirror. "I need your help," Matt spoke to the reflector as he set his hand onto the frame. "Please take us to Dash." Soon the aura pulled them through.

When they arrived to their requested destination, a cool punishing wind blew against their shaven faces.

"Dang, it's cold here!" Nick zipped his jacket until it went past his neck to his chin.

"Yea," Wrek agreed, "but where's here?"

They looked around and observed the tall trees, the playground equipment, and a gazebo. "We're in a park."

They walked past a restroom facility toward the highway that ran through the center of town. Nick looked in both directions. "I don't see any mountains."

The go-getters crossed the highway and advanced onto Main Street. They walked the sidewalk until they came to the library and read the sign. "Ancta, North Dakota. Wow, no wonder it's cold," Matt spoke.

They continued on past an arcade, across a side street to the small grocery store where they stood, taking in the pint-sized town.

"Okay," Wrek asked, "Now what?"

"We need to look for Dash's old beat-up truck."

"It's too cold. We need to go home and get warmer clothes." Wrek caught sight of the temperature on the bank's display panel before he led the way into the warm post office.

"What's Dash's last name? We could look in the phone book for his relative's address. He can't just be HERE in Aneta on his own."

"Good idea Nick, but I didn't see a pay phone anywhere."

Matt, Wrek, and Nick walked next door to Stove's Market where they bought sodas and searched the telephone directory.

"Is there someone I could help you find?" Mr. Stove asked them.

Matt looked at the store owner. "Yes, the Bradly's."

"Bradly's Inn?" he questioned. "They own the inn over on Fifth and Thayer."

After Mr. Stove pointed the way, the three men left the sotre. They walked around to the rear of the building where Matt closed his eyes and communicated with the mystical mirror through his mind.

Tuesday morning arrived. Matt gathered his long underwear, wool socks, and a knit hat before he went to see if Wrek and Nick were ready. As he entered the living room, he heard a knock at the front door. He stepped to the closed structure and peeked through the peephole. "Damn it!" he lipped when he saw the two detectives from Phoenix standing on his porch. He turned around and sped to his bedroom where he beseeched Dominique.

She looked straight into his wanton eyes. "Why would I want to talk to them?"

"I need you to woman. And if they ask, I'm not here."

Matt stood in the open doorway of his bedroom listening while his wife advanced to the main entrance of the house and opened the door. "Can I help you?" she asked softly.

"We're looking for Wrek Kerr. Is he here?"

She didn't want to lie more than what she had to. "I think so, come on in." She widened the space between the door and them.

The detectives entered and waited by the door while Dominique walked off and fetched her brother.

Wrek soon emerged into the living room and as he neared, he recognized and dreaded talking to his two visitors.

"First of all," Detective Justice reprimanded, "we didn't appreciate you leaving the hospital without further talking to us."

"I'm sorry," he falsely represented, "but I didn't feel like talking." He sat onto the love seat and invited the plain clothed officers to sit on the couch.

"We do understand your pain and the situation, but we need to ask you some questions."

Dominique returned to her husband, but stood silent in the hallway.

"What do you want to know?" Wrek asked.

"Nisa was your girlfriend?"

He nodded.

"We know about her kidnapping and that she owed Paul money. What do you know about that?"

"My sister provided the money, but sometime before I left the house to take the money to Nisa, an old friend of Matt's found out about it, snuck into our house, and switched briefcases on us. He was the one who suggested the bomb, but Matt told him no way, that he would rather sacrifice the money. Your murderer lives in Smelterville or at least he did." It felt good to his soul to nark on Dash since Nisa couldn't.

The detectives looked puzzled. "Who is Matt's old friend?"

He boldly gazed at them from across the coffee table. "Dash Bradly."

Detective Justice wrote in her notebook. "How did Matt know him?"

"He was in prison with him."

"And what do you mean 'or at least he did live in Smelterville?'"

"Matt and I went out to Dash's trailer and he was gone. He had packed up and moved."

Detective Kribz turned to his partner. "Maybe we should get a warrant and go search that trailer."

Laura wrote the address on her note pad, then cast her eyes again on Wrek. "Is Matt the guy who was at the hospital with you?"

He nodded.

Before the investigators left, they requested proof of Dominique's money transaction and informed Wrek they would be in town for a day or two.

Wrek closed and locked the front door. He then went to his sister's bedroom. "You heard?"

"Yea," Matt answered as he opened the bedroom door and stepped out. "Let's go get Dash and bring him here. We'll turn him over to those detectives and be done with it."

"Sounds good," Wrek agreed, then lit a cigarette.

The three sleuths soon met in the laundry room with their winter wear and manacles. Matt lit a joint and shared it before they faded through the mirror to North Dakota.

Detectives Justice and Kribz obtained a warrant, made phone calls to various rental agencies, then drove to Smelterville with Detective Amy from Wallace where they easily located the address given. The agent was already on the property inside the vacant rental house.

Laura, Steven, and Amy stepped in through the open door to the living room and greeted the landlord who was busy inspecting the condition of the dwelling.

"Is this where Dash's sister lived?" Laura asked.

"Yes and Dash stayed in the small trailer out back."

"Is it unlocked?"

"No." The landlord took hold of the keys and led the way out the door, upon the cement patio, and across the lawn to the small camper trailer.

The detectives entered the old establishment. "Phew! It smells in here."

Detective Amy stood in the open doorway and acted as an official witness. She observed the two out-of-state investigators stepping to the counter where they each reached into the forensic kit and grabbed a pair of latex gloves.

"Okay Wrek," Steven spoke aloud, "We're here to prove your accusations." He turned on the light and while he snapped a few photographs, Laura dusted the mini table for fingerprints. She lifted two impressions with clear adhesive tape and Steven then pulled out drawers and searched cupboards, looking for anything that could be used to make a bomb.

"Bingo!" Laura remarked as she inspected the floor underneath the table. "We have a piece of wire." She secured the metal conductor with her large tweezers and dropped it into a small plastic bag, then labeled it. "We'll send this to the crime lab for comparison."

Matt, Wrek, and Nick again arrived within the Aneta park. The wind wasn't as aggressive as yesterday, but the chill remained.

"Which way is Fifth Street?"

"I'm guessing that way." Matt gestured and led them away from the highway.

"By the way Matt," Wrek bid. "What's the plan?"

"Action is the plan," he firmly stated.

"Seriously. What's your plan? Dash just isn't going to go peacefully with us."

"Well, I called Bradly's Inn a few hours ago. There's no vacancy."

"Then how are we going to get into the building and nab Dash?"

"We'll have Nick distract the front counter person while we sneak in and hopefully," Matt paused as he took in a breath, "Dash or his sister ain't in the office."

"What am I suppose to say to them?" Nick questioned.

"Think of something," Wrek replied, "You want to be a bounty hunter, right?"

"Maybe."

As they neared the bushes that outlined the edge of the park, they caught sight of an old gray truck speeding through the uncontrolled four-way. "Is that him?" Their hearts were beating fast with eagerness, but Matt's was pumping with anger.

The three men stepped out onto the side street and cast their attention in the direction of the hurried vehicle. They walked to the next block and came upon a large two story prairie style house. Matt read the words from the signboard. "Bradly's Inn."

They saw Dash's truck parked within a row of leafless trees that were parallel to the white house. Matt was sly as he led the way behind the bushes and trees. He had Wrek and Nick stand guard within the small forest while he crept to the aged truck, lifted the hood, and quickly pulled the coil wire. He then returned to his partners. "Okay Nick, go!"

Nick adjusted his beanie hat to his eyebrows as he neared the building. He went through the entrance door and scanned the foyer, then stepped up to the desk to ask if there were any rooms available.

Inside the inn, Dash descended from the staircase and after he rounded the corner, he suddenly stopped when he recognized Nick's voice and stature. "What the hell is he doing here?" he spoke softly to himself as he stepped backwards around the same corner. He perceived that Matt and possibly Wrek also could be near. He darted up the stairway to his room.

Nick left the building and returned to Matt and Wrek. "No rooms and no sign of Dash or his sister."

"Okay—good. Go back in and ask where the nearest motel is," Matt proposed.

He willingly yielded to the request and walked again toward the large house, but this time, Matt and Wrek followed.

Dash stuffed his pockets with some of the stolen cash, slipped his jacket on, and cracked open his bedroom door. He was alert as he poked his head into the hallway and made his way to the rear exit.

Nick re-entered the inn with the two slinkers trailing. While he went into the office, Matt and Wrek hunched down and passed by the office window until they entered a hallway.

"Now what?" Wrek whispered as they stood upright.

Matt gestured for him to follow.

Dash exited through the back door and jogged around the corner of the house to his vehicle. He jumped into the cab, inserted the key, and attempted to start the engine. After no combustion, he stepped out and looked under the hood.

Matt led Wrek down the hall, all the while knocking on a few doors. No one answered at the first two rooms, however, at the third door, an elderly man answered. Wrek stood out of the way while Matt spoke. "Housekeeping. Do you need any towels?"

"No, I don't," the man grumbled and closed the door.

The two prowlers arrived at the end of the corridor where there was a window. Matt peered out. "There he is!"

Wrek took a glance and saw Dash inspecting under his truck's hood.

"Let's go!" Matt spoke as he swiftly backtracked through the corridor. He tried to lower himself as he hastened by the office window, then sped out the entry door.

Nick was standing on the porch smoking a cigarette when his stepfather and uncle raced by. He chased after them, hoping they had spotted their culprit.

Matt was in the lead, but only by a foot. Thoughts of what Dash had done to his sister and wife swept through his mind. He recently learned of a biological sister and now, she's gone before he could get to know her.

Dash heard a sudden rush of movement and cast his attention toward the direction of the stampede. "Oh shit!" he exclaimed when he saw Matt, Wrek, and Nick closing in on him. He gyrated and took off running, but couldn't run far, a tall fence blocked his way. He jumped and grabbed onto the ledge of the wooden barrier, then swung his right leg up and over.

Matt lunged at Dash. He seized his left leg while Wrek clutched onto his wrist. Together they yanked their man to the ground.

"You're not going anywhere!" Matt vented.

On his back, Dash fought back. He kicked Matt in the gut, thrusting him backwards to the ground. Dash quickly arose to his feet.

Wrek and Nick had him cornered against the fence, however, when he darted forward, Wrek grabbed his arm, but too much force, he broke loose and made his escape.

Nick gave chase with Wrek and Matt following.

"Run Nick!" Wrek shouted, "Use those young legs."

Dash sprinted, looking back as his pursuers closed in on him. He bolted through a grove of trees and came upon a large rock pile. He went around the heap and as he sat to rest, he pulled out and exposed a knife.

The three chasers stopped when they saw the sharp metal. Just four feet away, they stood gasping for air and wondered what to do next.

"What was that you said to me?" Dash looked at Matt with an evil eye. "You're not going to touch me!" He waved his blade to secure his threat.

"Bla, bla, bla. It's either us or the law."

"Go get the cops then."

Matt was silent, for Dash had called his bluff. He knew the police would side with Dash right now because they had no proof of his crime to arrest him nor were there any nationwide warrants issued.

Nick stood partially hidden behind Wrek. He slowly pulled from his jacket pocket, his slingshot and a large marble. He fixed the weapon onto his right arm and placed the stone into the leather pouch.

"No cops huh?" Dash jeered. "Give me back my coil wire."

"I tossed it." Matt saw out of the corner of his eye, what Nick was doing.

"Where?"

As Nick stepped out from behind Wrek, he lifted his arm, pulled the rubber cord backwards, and let the marble fly.

"Oh fuck!" Dash roared as he put his hand to his injury.

Matt and Wrek leaped and threw themselves onto their aggressor. Matt pressed his knee onto Dash's forearm until he released the knife while Wrek seized and held onto the other arm.

"Get the handcuffs!" Matt commanded to Nick. "They're in my back pocket."

"You have no right doing this to me!" Dash yelled.

"I have every right. You fucked my wife and killed my sister!" Matt's face boiled with anger. "You're going to turn yourself in."

Nick was shocked when he heard Matt's words.

"Roll him over," Wrek strongly bid.

Nick moved the knife out of harms way while Matt and Wrek struggled to get Dash turned over. Nick then slapped a cuff onto one of his wrists and as he waited for them to bring the other arm closer, he observed a red truck cruising slowly on the nearby dirt road. "I think we have company." He looked down and secured the other cuff.

As Matt stood, he glanced at the vehicle that was now stopped. He and Wrek took Dash by the arms and upthrew him to his feet. He then turned his attention to the powers of the mirror and instantly, green sparks appeared and one by one, they were vaporized and taken.

"Impressive," Dash commented with sarcasm after they arrived to the inside of the laundry room.

Matt and Wrek each lit a cigarette and forced their prisoner to sit on the bench.

"What? No cigarette for me?"

"You don't deserve one," Matt replied as Wrek stuck one in between Dash's lips anyways and lit it for him.

They took off their jackets and Nick left the room. He walked into the kitchen where the aroma of ham and baked beans wafted. "We're back," he said to his mom, then told her about their venture.

After noticing Dash's jacket was bulged, Matt sat on the bench next to him and searched his pockets. "Dominique's money?" he spoke as he pulled out a packet and looked at Dash. "Where's the rest of it?"

"Possibly back in his motel room," Wrek presumed.

Matt confiscated half of the money from his pocket and left the other half to prove to the detectives that he had taken it. "Let's go." Matt and Wrek walked Dash out to the carport and climbed into Matt's truck. They drove to the neighboring motel where Detectives Laura Justice and Steven Kribz took custody of Nisa's murderer.

TWENTY TWO

ROOM TWENTY

THE SEVEN FAMILY members sat around the dining table eating the ham and baked beans.

Wrek loaded a quarter of his plate with potato salad while Matt buttered a roll. Dominique poured her milk as well as Ian's.

"Watch those beans Uncle Wrek—You get gassy!" Travis reported.

"I'll be sure to stand by you when it hits," he teased.

There was a pause from the chatter. Only the clinging of forks and grinding of food was heard. "Hey Nick?" Matt broke the silence. "Thanks for helping today. You're going to make a great bounty hunter someday."

"Yes, he is," Dominique agreed as she looked up from her plate, "from what I hear."

Soon enough, the boys finished eating and left the table.

"Boy, I'm tired." Wrek yawned as he observed the darkness through the dining room window. "I'm gonna go take a nap." He arose and carried his plate into the kitchen before heading to his bedroom.

"What about you?" Dominique asked her husband who was lighting a cigarette. "Are you tired?"

He nodded. "My gut hurts a little from where Dash kicked me."

"I'm glad he's gone," she spoke as she eyed the faint black hair and structure of her husband's forelimb, wanting to hold his hand again. "He didn't turn out to be a very good friend."

"Once a con, always a con," he replied with a downcast frame of mind. "And I'm not looking forward to his trial."

She forced a half smile, then embraced his hand.

Matt tightened the grip, aching to be touched as well, but too afraid to say so. "I know it wasn't your fault." He inhaled a drag from his cigarette. It was as though he wanted to say more, but didn't know what.

"I'm just going to forget about what happened, you're the only one I want to be with," she asserted.

"It's going to be hard to forget. The thought of him inside of you burns me up."

"We'll just have to pray about it."

Matt let go of her hand, arose from his chair, and walked to the kitchen. He stepped to the refrigerator and took hold of a beer. He retired to his bedroom and Dominique loaded the dishwasher.

Nathan knocked on Travis' bedroom door, then entered. He closed the wooden structure, stepped to, and sat on the floor by his brother who was playing his video game system.

"What's up?" Travis asked as he continued pressing buttons on the controller.

"I overheard Uncle Wrek and Matt talking about mom's money. The money that Dash stoled."

"Yea?" His blue eyes brightened with curiosity. "Go on."

"All I know is, it's in Dash's room where ever they went to through the mirror."

"What's your point?"

"What's my point? Let's go get this leftover money for ourselves."

Travis pushed pause and turned his attention more to what Nathan was saying.

"We can buy lots of stuff: candy, pop, dirty magazines."
He spoke covertly towards Travis' ear.

"How do we know where to go?"

"Nick knows."

The two young teenagers stood to their feet and crept to
Nick's bedroom. They eagerly, but quietly knocked.

"Come in."

They entered.

"What do you want?"

"We need to talk to you about something," Nathan said
while they stepped in and shut the door.

Nick was comfortably sitting on his bed with his pillows
propped behind him. He pressed the volume button on his
remote control to lower the sound of his television.

Travis seated himself onto Nick's beanbag chair and
Nathan sat on the carpeted floor. "I overheard Uncle Wrek
and Matt talking about mom's money that Dash stoled. We
need your help to go get it."

"I'm too tired right now."

"Tomorrow?"

"Sure, but we're splitting it fifty-fifty. You two have to
share a fifty."

PPLLL! Nathan ripped a vapor as he lifted a butt cheek.

"Eeww!" Travis roared with a sour expression upon his face.

"No farting in my room!" Nick firmly ruled.

"Sorry—it's the beans from dinner."

The clock struck ten A.M. Nathan and Travis were
anxious to venture through the mirror; they just had to wait
for Nick to stir. They stood fully dressed in the hallway.
Nathan leaned in by Nick's closed door and forced a cough.
Travis stepped in and gave one knock, then scurried to his
room. Nathan quickly followed.

"We need Ian," Travis suggested, "Nick won't get mad at
him for waking him up."

At that moment, Dominique ascended the staircase to give
hugs and discuss their chores. "Are your bedrooms clean?"

"No," they answered.

"I want them spotless. Beds made with clean sheets, vacuum, dust, take your dirty clothes to the laundry room, then I want you to help Nick take down the trampoline and stack the pieces nicely inside the garage. It's the middle of November; too cold to jump."

"Then can we be free for the rest of the day?"

"Yes. I'll wake Nick for you."

Travis and Nathan looked at each other and smiled.

It was twelve o'clock when Nathan, Travis, and Nick finished their work. Nick nuked himself a corndog while his two brothers gathered a backpack, jackets, gloves and hats.

Wrek left for work and Matt was at his mother's house. Ian carried his box of small plastic horses to the natatorium where his mom waited for him. Dominique was already in the water, engaging in her arobics. With his life jacket and foam board, he set his collection of toy animals afloat.

Nathan stepped into the pool area and informed his mother that he was going to Sandy's and Travis was leaving too.

"Check in in a few hours," she called out.

He went to the laundry room where he joined Travis and Nick. He closed the door and slipped his jacket on. Nick caressed the mirror's frame while he talked to it. "Beautiful and candid mirror, please take us three pups to Aneta, North Dakota for two hours." The speculum activated and they were pulled through.

The money seekers stood in the empty gazebo within the park. They scanned the area and observed younger kids oscillating on the swings.

"Let's sit here for a minute," Nick proposed as he lit a cigarette. "Don't tell mom."

"It's your lungs," Travis forewarned.

The sound of the childrens' laughter spread throughout the acre, followed by a semi truck passing slowly along the highway.

"I wonder how much money is in Dash's room?" Nathan marveled at the thought.

"We'll soon find out." Nick arose, dropped his half cigarette to the floorboard, and pressed the hot tip with the forepart of his shoe. They headed toward Fifth Street.

They walked at an easy pace and soon came upon the big white house; Bradly's Inn. Dash's truck remained parked in the same spot and the signboard on the property now read vacancy. They advanced to the backside of the trees, then stopped.

"The office lady knows me so I can't be seen. You two go to the office and ask what room Dash stays in, then go to the rear exit and let me in."

While Nathan and Travis moved to carry out their task, Nick crossed the back yard toward the rear door of the building. He breathed a quick breath to ease his nerves as he neared and reached for the knob.

Nathan and Travis entered the office and as they stepped to the receptionist, they removed their hats. Afraid, but showing courage, Travis spoke. "We're looking for Dash. Could you tell us what room he's staying in?"

With a suspicious glare, the gray haired woman asked why.

"He wanted us to do some work for him."

She forced a smile and spoke politely. "Sure. Room twenty. It's on the second floor."

"Thank you." Nathan replied as they turned away. He led the way out to the foyer and through the hall.

The woman had doubt about the two boys since she was Dash's mother and knew her son was last seen yesterday afternoon. She lifted the receiver to the telephone and dialed for the local sheriff.

Nathan and Travis met Nick at the back door and let him in. They scaled the staircase to room twenty and entered. They closed and locked the door, then began searching for the money.

Nathan set his backpack onto the bed and knelt to the floor. While he spied underneath the bed, Nick looked in the closet and Travis rummaged through the dresser drawers.

"Nothing." Still on his knees, Nathan brought his head to pillow level, sat on his heels, and took in the unique design of the bed frame. "Hmm . . . I wonder?" He lifted the skirt of the blue striped comforter, then heaved the edge of the top mattress. There lying on the box spring was the legal tender.

Nick and Travis bolted over to the bed and dropped to their knees. Nick snatched the backpack, unzipped it, and spread open the mouth.

With his arm, Travis swooped the heap of cash into the lightweight bag and Nick zipped it. "We can count it later— we need to get out of here," he stressed.

Nathan lowered the mattress into place and they stood to their feet.

Nick placed the backpack onto his back and stepped to the door where he unlocked and cracked it open. He peeked out. "The coast is clear," he whispered.

The trespassers quietly left the room and shut the door. They walked with wary steps within the hallway and down the stairs. They made their escape through the rear exit of the house, then conquered the back lot and row of trees.

Travis glanced at his watch. "We still have over an hour to wait."

"Let's go back to the gazebo."

Nick, Travis, and Nathan rested on the benches inside of the belvedere. Nick removed the knapsack from his back and tossed it to Nathan. "You can hold it." He then lit a cigarette.

Nathan bent forward, unfastened and opened the backpack, then took a peek. "I feel badly." He selected a packet and held it within the bag. "This is mom's money. We should just give it back to her." He let the cash drop down to its buddies.

Travis surveyed the park. The swings hung bare and the slide echoed the sun's reflection. He observed a white car traveling upon the highway, then turning onto the street that led closest to them. "Oh shit!" he uttered as the vehicle journeyed closer. "It's a cop." A look of worry grew upon his face as he turned and cast his eyes in the direction of his brothers.

When the sheriff's car stopped alongside the curb and parked, Nick discreetly tossed his pack of cigarettes into a nearby bush, then butted the tobacco stick he was smoking. "Don't say anything about the mirror or the money," he cautioned.

With his foot, Nathan slid the backpack underneath the bench where he sat.

The sheriff walked the sidewalk toward them. "Good afternoon boys." He ceased at the step and stood tall and firm.

"Hello," Travis and Nathan replied, but not Nick.

"I received a call that you three could be up to some mischief?"

The boys sat quiet.

"Where do you live?" The officer eyed Nick.

Nick sat restlessly as he gave thought to escaping. If I could just stay hidden for an hour, he pondered, the mirror will take us home and we'll be rid of this pig. "Does it matter?" he answered with a saucy tongue.

Nathan and Travis' eyes widened with strong interest. They glanced at the officer, at Nick, then again at the policeman.

"Yes it does matter," the officer returned as he gestured with his finger for Nick to step over to him.

"We live in Idaho!" Nathan blurted.

The sheriff took the two steps up to the floorboard of the gazebo and advanced to Nick.

Nick stood.

The officer turned Nick around. "Put your hands on top of your head and spread your legs."

He complied.

The sheriff kept an eye on Travis and Nathan as he patted Nick down. He pulled from his back pocket a wallet, then extracted his driver's license. "You can sit down." He looked over the information. "Are you staying at Bradly's Inn?" He awaited their answer, knowing they weren't.

"No."

"Why were you inside the building?"

"We were looking for a friend. Is there a law against that?" Nick expressed in a scornful manner.

"No law against that, but there is a law against trespassing and if you keep up your attitude, I might charge you with it."

Nick looked away.

The sheriff turned to Nathan. "Are you three brothers?"

"Yea." He looked at the lawman with his big worrisome eyes, hoping he wouldn't ask to see the backpack.

"Who are you staying with?"

They were silent.

"Okay . . ." He frowned. "Where's your parents?"

"Our mom is at home."

"Did you guys run away?"

"We have the right to remain silent," Travis stated.

"But you're not under arrest." He suspected something wasn't right. "Come with me." He escorted them to his car where he ordered Nathan and Travis to sit on the back seat and Nick in the front. "Put your seatbelts on. It's about thirty miles to the station."

Dominique sat at her desk, writing on her second novel. She took hold of her stereo remote and pressed the skip button; it went to the next song. Ian was playing with his wrestling figures upon his little table. He had the ring set up and his accessories scattered. Wrek entered from the kitchen.

"I thought you were at work?" Dominique turned an eye toward her brother.

His appearance was that of a gloomy gus who didn't get what he wanted for Christmas. "They let me come home. I couldn't concentrate." He parked himself onto the couch.

Dominique continued with her writing into the next song.

"That song reminds me of Nisa." He took a quick toke from his marijuana pipe.

"Every song is going to remind you of her." She didn't want to, but empathy made her press the button for the next lyric.

He exhaled his swell of smoke. "I miss my minikin. I really loved her." With his red and puddled eyes, he let a few tears run down his cheeks.

"Uncle Wrek's crying," Ian indicated to his mom as he watched his male elder with wonder.

Wrek grabbed a sofa pillow. "Crying for Nisa," he clarified, then put the soft cushion to his face to muffle his sounds.

The telephone rang. Dominique muted her stereo and answered the call. By the time the conversation ended, she was baffled. She turned to her brother who had wiped his face and composed himself. "Guess where the boys are?"

"Uh-oh." He sensed the mirror had something to do with this.

She arose from her chair and stomped to the laundry room. Ian raced after her. She seized a blanket from the closet and when she covered the glass to the reflector, she heard it growl. "No more!" she vented, "No more mirror!" She wrenched herself around, turned off the light, and closed the door.

"Come on Ian. We have stuff to do." She telephoned Matt at his mother's house, requesting his assistance, then she went to Ian's bedroom and gathered some of his clothes. She went to her bedroom and packed a suitcase. "We're going on a long drive to go free your brothers from jail, so go grab Duhe, your pillow, and a few of your small toys."

"Can I grab my blanket?"

"Please do."

TWENTY THREE

DOMINIQUE'S MISADVENTURE

THE RIDE HOME from North Dakota was cramped. Nick, Travis, and Nathan occupied the back seat and Ian sat in the front between his mom and Matt. They had just driven over the Montana border, traveling west down Lookout Pass into Idaho.

Emotions were mixed. Dominique wasn't happy that her boys had missed three days of school and snuck through the mirror after lieing about their intentions, however, she was grateful they had retrieved most of her money.

"How long are we grounded for?"

"As long as it takes," she barked.

They were soon home. They exited the car and stretched their sore bodies. "Oh my butt hurts." Matt opened the trunk and grabbed the suitcase and Nathan's backpack. Dominique took hold of Ian's belongings while the boys carried their jackets. They advanced to the front door and entered the house.

"Uncle Wrek? We're home." Ian shouted for, but was no where to be found.

"It's good to be home," they all agreed.

"Mom—I'm sorry." Nathan stepped in for a hug. "We should of told you."

"If we told her," Nick added, "she wouldn't of let us go."

Dominique returned the embrace. "That's probably true, or I would of sent Wrek with you."

Nick headed upstairs to go shower and change his clothes. Travis soon followed, then Nathan.

Dominique took a late afternoon siesta. When she awoke, it was almost five. She arose, slipped her jeans and pink bunny slippers on, then went to the kitchen where she gathered dinner. Soon the expanse smelt of corn dogs and tator tots.

Matt came in from the garage. "You're up." He stepped to his wife and kissed her.

"You smell like gas."

"I was messing with my dirt bike."

She butted her cigarette and lit the joint she had stashed in her cigarette pack.

After dinner, Nick and Nathan returned to their bedrooms. Even though Dominique protested because darkness had prevailed, Matt took Ian for a short ride on his dirt bike.

Travis followed his mom into the laundry room. "My show will be on in five minutes," he complained.

"It will only take four minutes to move this mirror to the garage." She flipped on the light, then fixed an angry stare on the masked imager. "I'm going to destroy that damn mirror!" She stepped to her tall swing glass and grabbed it at the centre claw. She gestured with a jerk of her head for Travis to take hold of the other end. As they attempted to lift the reflector, the blanket fell to the floor. Sparks flew. Dominique's raction was to snatch Travis' arm and run out of the room, but the mirror exerted its force and in an instant, they disappeared through the glass surface.

Dominique and Travis landed on their hands and knees upon the cold linoleum floor inside a building. They heard a man yelling. "Hurry up! Put it all in the bag." The tone of his voice was rough.

Dominique was struck with sudden fear. A quick survey of the expanse confirmed they were in a bank. She looked at her son and placed her index finger to her lips, instructing him to be quiet.

They were out of view of the aggressive man. Her heart was pounding as she crawled to the nearby kiosk with Travis in pursuit of her. They stayed hidden while they sat. She parted her lips to quiet her breathing.

Coins were dropped onto the floor from the cashiers' station. "Open the fuckin' drawer!"

The teller pleaded for her safety.

Dominique and Travis then heard the sound of bullets being sprayed onto the ceiling and walls, breaking light bulbs and damaging cameras.

The bank clerk squealed.

Matt and Ian entered the house from the garage. With a smile on his face, Ian went dashing through the kitchen into the living room. "Mom?" he called out, but only found Wrek walking in the hallway towards his bedroom. "Do you know where my mommy is?"

"No—I just got home."

Both Matt and Ian searched for Dominique upstairs, in her bedroom, the bathrooms, and the natatorium.

"Maybe she's doing the laundry." Matt advanced to the laundry room. When he stepped in, the light was on and he observed a blanket lying on the floor in front of the cheval mirror. "Hmm?" He bent over and picked up the woven material and draped it upon the mirror. He turned off the light and exited the room.

Ian opened the front door and with just a shirt and jeans, he stepped out to the cold night air and peeked at the driveway. He rushed back into the warm house and slammed the door. "Her car is still here."

Dominique glanced at the clock again. It was almost six. She and Travis had been hiding for two minutes, however, it felt like ten. She turned her vigilant eyes to the doorway. It was too far away to risk trying to escape. She closed her eyes and tried to communicate with the mystical mirror, but to no avail, it didn't work.

The masked gunman forced the teller to the lobby where he ordered her to lie on the floor next to her frightened colleagues. He instructed them to keep their faces to the ground and count to a hundred before anyone looked up. He lifted his fully automatic weapon and fired a few rounds into the air as he backed away toward the doors. With his bag of loot, the six foot one bank robber gyrated and exited the building, running off into the darkness.

Through the assemblage of the glass, Dominique could see no sign of law enforcement, only the headlights of the sparse traffic. She didn't want to hang around and try to explain how she arrived at the bank, so she motioned for Travis to follow her. She uplifted to her feet, but stayed at a squat. She peeked around the kiosk and seen that the employees were still faced down. She straightened her legs and as she tiptoed in her bunny slippers to the door, she kept her identity hidden.

Dominique and Travis hastened upon the sidewalk away from the bank. She caught a quick look at the bank's electronic display panel and noted the forty-nine degree temperature. "A little warmer than Kellogg," she breathed.

Travis who wore a hooded sweat shirt and sports shorts, followed his mother to the next block. They rounded the edge of a brick building and stopped.

"You think we're safe now?" Travis asked.

"I hope so." Dominique scanned the unfamiliar territory. The night sky twinkled with bright stars, however, the local vicinity seemed to be the dark area of town. She could see from the street light, an old building across the roadway that displayed graffiti. The slang and obscene words confirmed there could be danger lurking.

She studied the direction of Lewis Street and saw a neon sign advertising a twenty-four hour convenient store. "There." She pointed. "We could go there and call Matt." They crossed the vacant street and walked a block before they detected the many cop cars now down the street at the bank.

They refocused and continued through the dark towards the store. They advanced to the end of the next block and became aware of an unlighted underpass they would have to travel to get to their destination. Just then, they heard faint voices. Voices that told them of intoxicated men whooping it up. Fear hit them. They halted in their steps and Dominique looked at her son. "We're not walking under there." She wasn't about to risk being harassed, raped, or worse, killed.

Dominique spun around as she searched for other possibilities. She noticed a small sign that announced a motel, then she crossed Lewis Street.

She and Travis neared the rundown establishment. They entered the scanty office and a swarthy woman with long black hair greeted them in a foreign language. "Buenas noches," she said.

Dominique didn't understand, however, she asked to use the telephone.

"No use phone. Policy," she spoke rudely.

Dominique and Travis returned to the outdoors, to the parking lot. "What a bitch," she remarked as they walked. "I need a cigarette."

"Light one up," Travis replied.

"I don't have any with me."

They approached Lewis Street once again and stood on the sidewalk. "We can't go that way." She cast her eyes toward the bank, then turned her head to the opposite direction. "Can't go that way, unless we want to be attacked. Our only option." She looked straight ahead. "Is forward and hopefully we run into a gas station or a store." They walked north on First Avenue.

Matt paced parallel to the bay window in the living room while Wrek sat and watched television. Nick and

Nathan descended and stood at the bottom of the staircase. "You find Mom and Travis yet?"

"No," Matt answered. His tone sounded like a man ready for action.

"Maybe we should call the cops?" One of the boys suggested.

"Not yet." He glanced at the clock on the wall above the threshold to the kitchen. "Six thirty. She's only been gone a half an hour."

Ian walked into the room. "Mom left her cigarettes on the counter." He placed the pack and her lighter onto the coffee table for everyone to see.

"Maybe she went next door to the neighbors?"

"I doubt it. They're older folks."

There was a pause in talk as the television broadcasted a soap commercial.

Nick spoke. "Do you think the mirror sent them somewhere?"

They all rushed to the laundry room. Matt insisted the three boys wait in the hallway while he stepped in and pulled the blanket from the mirror to the floor. He stood with his arms crossed against his throbbing chest as he glared at the imager. "Okay mirror!" he spoke solid, "Where did you send my wife and stepson to?"

Dominique rubbed the goosebumps on her arms, trying to keep warm as she and Travis walked the sidewalk on First Avenue. They crossed Clark Street and walked by a small house that was pedaling Latino music. The residential area seemed to resemble that of a Spanish-speaking community.

When they approached the proximity of a neighboring yard, Dominique was startled and jumped away because a dog had raced to the fence and barked.

"Chico?" The owner called for his Chihuahua from the lighted porch of his casa.

She and Travis stepped up their pace, by-passing more houses and a high-rise building. "Mom, do you think we're in Mexico?"

"No. The street signs are in English and the bank robber spoke English."

They came to the next block. Dominique skimmed her vision up and down the dark street. "Oh no," she mumbled, then Travis also observed a number of hoodlums four or five yards away.

Through the moonlight, they watched one of the men kick on a mailbox as his buddies cheered him on.

"We have to get out of here." Dominique barely spoke; fear had clogged her throat.

The hombres appeared to be advancing their way. Travis and Dominique turned back and fled.

"I think they saw us," Travis' voice quivered.

They raced a half block, then darted into an alley and stopped suddenly. "Wait," Dominique cautioned, "People get killed in alleyways."

"What do you want to do then?"

While she scanned the dark passageway, they heard heavy footsteps drawing near. "Let's hide." They leaped and knelt behind a Dumpster. She took in a few deep breaths, then seperated her lips to calm her breathing. "I feel like I'm gonna puke," she whispered to Travis.

"You can't, they will hear you."

She had her arms wrapped around her stomach. "My nerves are shot—I can't take any more drama."

"It'll be okay Mom," he consoled as he placed his hand onto her back and patted.

The clatter of the men was upon them. They stood in the dark alleyway smoking their cigarettes. "Where'd they go ese?" one of them asked in his Spanish accent.

"They ran away," his buddy replied.

"No. I bet they're hiding somewhere." The eager fellow eyed the Dumpster. "Possibly behind this garbage bin."

Dominique and Travis' hearts began to pound with extreme fear.

A car entered into the lane with its bright headlights shining their way. The roguish pack recognized the automobile to be a police vehicle so they turned and fled.

Dominique and Travis remained hidden while the patrol car slowly cruised the alleyway. When it was clear, they arose to their feet and dashed to the opposite end of the passageway where they beheld, two blocks away, a second convenience store. "Thank God!" she praised as they started walking.

Soon they arrived at the small retail store and stepped inside. "It's warmer in here," Dominique spoke low to Travis while she cast her eyes about the enclosure.

"Can I help you find something?" The cashier asked her.

"A telephone."

"Outside." He pointed to a corner towards the rear of the building.

Oh great, she thought, back outside into the cold. "Could you tell me what city I'm in?"

"Pasco, Washington." He gave her an odd look. "There's a police station and hospital right down the road."

She thanked the attendant, then advanced to the parking lot and to the pay phone.

Matt was scolding the quiescent mirror when he heard the telephone ring. "I'll get it!" he called out as he spun himself around and leaped out of the laundry room.

After he lifted the receiver and said hello, he was relieved as he conversed with his wife. "I'll try to see if the mirror will pull you through now that I know where you're at. If it doesn't work, I'll be there with the car in about three hours."

Dominique bummed a cigarette from a man who was pumping gas, then she and Travis walked toward the hospital. "We can wait in the lobby where it's warm." While they walked the sidewalk, a green haze came about, then they were swallowed up into the nimbus to home.

TWENTY-FOUR

BLACK FOG

Travis bragged of the bank robbery and the other happenings to his brothers over the weekend and Dominique stayed in bed. Come Monday morning, Travis was back at school with Nathan while Dominique traveled with Matt and Ian to Spokane. Wrek had to work and Nick went to his GED class.

Matt drove into the parking lot of the federal building and they exited the car.

"Why are we here Mamma?"

"Matt has to go see the judge. He got a ticket." She held onto his hand while they walked inside the large structure and up the stairwell.

Matt located the correct courtroom and entered the formal area ahead of his wife and five year old stepson. After awhile, Ian was having trouble sitting still, so his mother escorted him out to the corridor.

Dominique sat on a bench across the entrance way of the courtroom near the elevator while Ian jumped in place, wanting to run. She periodically arose and stepped to the small window in the door for a peek at Matt. After the third time, she turned around to check on Ian and he was gone.

She quickly searched up the corridor, then down. "Oh no!" she groaned to herself.

As she advanced toward the elevator, she noticed from the buttons, the boxed unit was descending. She pressed the round disk to bring it back up. She was fearful that someone was attempting to kidnap her child. There was no time to waste, the mechanical platform was taking too long. Panic set in and she rushed to the stairwell where she made tracks to the first floor. The elevator door had just closed. She pushed the button, but the device moved upward. She scanned the proximity and saw four people, none of them were Ian.

Dominique raced up the three flight of stairs and as she waited for the elevator, she gasped for air. She watched the buttons and detected they weren't lighting up. She stood and waited in front of the closed door. Within a minute, she heard a faint call. She leaned her ear in towards the crack.

"Mommy?"

"Ian?" she implored as she put her mouth to the cleft, then returned to listening.

"Mommy!?" Ian bleated out.

She was thrilled to know where he was, but now she had a new problem; her little boy was trapped inside the elevator. "Is anyone in there with you?"

"No . . ."

"Push the number three on the buttons," she instructed.

"I'm too scared." He began to whimper. "Get me out of here!"

"Don't be scared Baby Zebra." What do I do? She asked herself.

It took the maintenance man ten minutes to unjumble and reset Ian's feat of button pushing. He apologized, then waited quietly with his mom until Matt was dismissed by the court.

They did some shopping in the city before heading back to Kellogg. Ian fell asleep on the way home and was carried into the house, into his bedroom, and placed onto his bed.

Dominique then walked to the kitchen where Matt was loading his pipe and while she stored the groceries away, she insisted he destroy that mirror.

That afternoon, Matt and Wrek transferred the mysterious imager out to the garage.

"Why can't we just give the mirror to someone else?"

"Come on Wrek, you know we can't do that—it's our problem, nobody else's."

They set the reflector onto its backside with the blanket still spread over the glass. Matt grabbed hold of his sledgehammer, heaved it into the air above his head, and swung it downward, hitting the covered exterior. As he pounded, only the groaning of the mirror was heard. They became curious.

While Wrek watched, Matt carefully pinched the edge of the blanket and when he brought it back, a bright light emitted from the unbroken speculum, accompanied by a high pitched whistle like that of a teakettle.

"Aahh . . . I'm blind!" Matt roared as he closed and put his hands over his eyelids.

Wrek also was visually impaired. "Cover the glass before it pulls us through!"

Matt went to his knees and groped for the blanket. After he shielded the reflector, he opened his watery eyes. His vision was blurred. He tried to focus in on Wrek and saw, just a dark figure. He lit a cigarette and smoked on it while he waited for his sight to return.

Wrek went to the tool cabinet and grasped onto an ax. He stepped beside the mirror, aimed, and took a swing at the center of the glass surface. As he raised the splitting tool, he noticed the metal tip was now flat. "Oh wow!" he expressed with amazement. "This mirror is unbreakable."

Matt paced as he gave thought. "Okay—it can't be disassembled. We'll . . ." He elevated his hands into the air, "burn it." They lifted and carried the imager to the cement driveway out behind the garage and into the alleyway.

Dominique approached and stepped in close to Matt who was knelt and flicking his lighter. She scanned the neighborhood since she thought it might seem odd to anyone watching for her husband to be setting a piece of furniture on fire.

Matt flicked his lighter and flicked it again. "It won't catch." He looked up at Wrek, then Dominique.

Wrek put his spontaneous idea into action. He rushed into the garage, seized the charcoal fluid, then returned to Matt and squirted some of the flammable liquid alongside the mahogany frame. He stepped back and Matt flashed his lighter. The wood of the mirror and the blanket erupted into flames.

"Oh . . . awesome!" they exclaimed.

All of a sudden, water shooted up from the glass and the fire went out. The mini geyser sprayed the three onlookers, soaking their hair and clothes. The fountain subsided, then pellets of hail spewed out, pelting their wet bodies and tender skin. They leaped away.

Dominique rushed into the house. She slipped her shoes off at the back door and while she walked to her bedroom, she felt the pain and swelling from the welts upon her entire body. With much care, she took off her wet clothes, then downed some ibuprofen. "Stupid mirror," she grumbled.

Matt and Wrek suffered through the pain. When the hailstorm ceased, they stepped to and examined the mirror. It was dry. "Amazing," Matt stated, "It's as good as new. There's no burn marks on it."

They picked up the imager and moved it back to the garage. While Matt stood and expressed a glare, a surge of anger came upon him. He stepped to the nearby shelf and grabbed a can of black paint. He shook the container, causing the steel ball to rattle the chemicals about, then he pointed the nozzle and sprayed the glass surface.

Matt and Wek positioned themselves a few feet away from the unpredictable piece of furniture and smoked on their cigarettes while they waited for something to happen.

Soon enough, the paint disappeared through the surface and the glass once again, echoed a bright reflection. "Hmm . . ." They butted their tobacco sticks, then Matt sprayed the shiny device once more.

Smoke blew from the mirror's interior, quickly filling the garage with a black fog. They were coughing as they leaped toward the door and when they opened the movable entry to air out the space, the mirror began to suck the dark fog back through itself. Their eyes widened with wonder while they watched the haze vanish. Matt soon closed the door and kept an inquiring eye on the imager as him and Wrek neared.

Immediately, a great many of winged insects flew out from the glass. "What the hell?" Matt shouted as he waved his arms about. They could barely keep their eyes open.

"The flies are everywhere." Wrek was trying to slap them away. "I have one up my nose!" He blew through his nostrils, but it just tickled. He then tried to pick the fly out with his finger and only made the sensation worse so he pinched his nose, squishing the insect.

Matt was hacking on one that had flown into his throat. He again raced toward the exit to escape into the back yard and Wrek followed, closing the door.

Wrek secured the edge of his shirt and blew his nose into it. "Oh gross!" he remarked to his brother-in-law as he showed him the bloody fly guts.

Matt acted as though he wanted to vomit. He turned away and hustled toward the house. After he entered through the rear door, he went to the refrigerator for a drink. He downed a pop, clearing his throat of any bugs, then he lit a cigarette. While he smoked, he examined his welts.

Wrek came inside the house and grabbed himself a drink as well. "You going back out there?" He took his shirt off.

"Of course I am, but first I'm gonna go check on Dominique and smoke a dober." He burped long and loud, then headed to his bedroom.

Some thirty minutes later, Matt and Wrek resurfaced into the kitchen wearing dry clothes. Nick joined them, anxious to watch. They decked themselves with sweatshirts and went outdoors.

Matt stepped to the garage and after he turned the knob, he slowly inched open the door and stuck his face through the gap to take a peek.

"Matt?"

He heard an eerie voice from within the enclosure speak his name. "Huh?" He cast his eyes about and saw no one.

"Mathew Jax?"

He closed the door and looked at Wrek. "The flies are gone. You go get the shovels."

Nick overheard. "What are you going to do?"

"Bury it," Matt replied. "Nothing else has worked."

Wrek returned from within the garage with the two shovels and handed one to his nephew.

"I just came out to watch."

Matt pounded his footfalls over to Nick and snatched the shovel from his hand.

"What's up with that?" Nick asked.

"You don't want to help," he thundered, then turned away and walked to a secluded corner of the yard where he started digging.

Wrek stepped to Matt, lifted his foot to the rim of the shovel, and stomped the tip into the ground. Together, they dug a seven by three feet hole, and yet deep enough to fit the imager.

Nick sat on the porch swing with his mom. She smoked on her cigarette and hoped the mirror would be buried before the boys came home from school. She didn't want them to know where it was at.

Matt and Wrek carried the strange reflector from the garage and dropped it into the cavity in the ground. With great haste, they scooped and heaved the dirt onto the glass. They filled the hole and patted the topsoil with the bottom of their shovels, then arranged the pieces of sod atop.

They stepped back and admired their work. Matt looked at Wrek. "Well—that's that!"

The ground beneath them bagan to shake. Matt and Wrek stood and watched in awe, just as Dominique and Nick did from the veranda. The earth opened and swallowed up a small tree and a few nearby bushes. It devoured the sod as the land churned its elements. Next came an uprush of dirt, stones, and roots expelling into the air and scattering. Through the dust and rubble, the mirror flew above their heads and landed on its long feet in front of Matt. He glanced at his wife and saw the unbelief in her wide blue eyes.

The volcanic action had settled and when Matt returned his vision onto the dusty glass, a powerful wind came forth from with the imager, blowing itself clean, then it knocked him to his rear.

"Listen to me!" the mirror's command vibrated through the wind.

Matt stared quietly at the reflector as he remained sitting. The stiff breeze immediately died out. He bounced a glimpse at his brother-in-law and gestured with a jerk of his head for him to draw near.

After Wrek approached him, he arose to his feet and dusted the dirt from his behind. "Help me carry this back to the garage."

They set the mirror in the far corner. "I've had enough, I'll be in the house." Wrek left and closed the door, leaving Matt alone with the wayward device.

"Matt?"

He heard that eerie vocal sound again. "Who are you?" His words trembled as he spoke.

"Don't you recognize my voice?"

He did. "This is so odd." He cast his attention upon the glass. "You're . . ." he hesitated, "You're passed on. You died three months ago."

"Only my body. I'm having a great time in my spirit; flying around in space, diving through the galaxies, chasing the angels—Don't tell your mom!"

Matt saw his father's face, a young version of his face, appear within the glass. He eagerly listened.

"It's beautiful out here. The stars are like gleaming jewels and sometimes the light from the stars reflect off the nearby dust and gases making the atmosphere purple and red. I've just recently visited Jupiter," Stanley added, "The renowned red spot is a remarkable carnival ride. I spent two days swirling the gaseous tornado."

"Awesome. What else have you been doing?"

"I met a few saints so far, Peter for one. He's a great guy to roll with. Last week, we were floating to the moon and on the way, we observed a shooting star. Peter tried to jump on, but it was traveling too fast."

Matt chuckled.

"The most breathtaking and mind-blowing of all this though, is seeing the Lord."

"I agree," he stated, then lit a cigarette. "I'm glad to be talking with you, but there has to be a reason why you're here?" He relaxed himself into a lawn chair that he placed in front of the mirror.

"True, there is."

"Are you the one who's been taking and sending us to different places?" Matt inquired.

"I had to. I needed you to save your sister."

"And that I did. Wrek and I, but then disaster came upon her."

"It's not your fault."

Matt reflected a moment to remember his twin sibling.

"I wanted to bring my first family together, the family that was torn from my control. You Matt—you were the only one I found after I was married to Jasmine, then in April of seventy-four, I learned your birth mother had died suddenly. I never knew Nisa, until recently."

Matt's face grew pale. He was speechless as he looked down at the floor.

"I never told your mom about Nisa or that you were my biological son. I didn't want to hurt her."

He lifted his eyes and glared at his father. "She knows. She read your secret letters that you kept hidden in the attic."

He cast his vision to the frame of the mirror, not wanting to stay within eye contact.

"Matt? I want to ask you for your forgiveness."

There was silence. Matt slouched forward in his chair as he puffed on his cigarette.

"I was mean to you, I was too tough and strict on both you and David. I should of talked to you more about your problems and encouraged you instead of hit on you."

A tear dripped from his eye that he quickly wiped away with his finger.

"I drove you to drinking," Stanley continued, "And that wasn't good—I'm sorry." His tone was sincere.

Matt let his cigarette drop to the floor, then he twisted the cherry out with the tip of his shoe.

"Before I go . . ."

Matt looked up.

"Before I go, I have your mother here with me. She wants to meet you."

"Oh my God," he cursed unknowingly. Sudden fear hit him. "Okay . . ." he stuttered as he anxiously watched for her to appear within the mirror.

"Hello my son."

He was pleasantly surprised to hear her angelic voice and to see her facial features. She was a beautiful Indian woman who resembled Nisa, then he told himself Nisa resembled her. Such a miracle, he thought, to be meeting his birth mother, especially in the manner he was, but then he would have to wait until he passed away to join them.

It was almost one in the morning when Matt said his farewells and went into the house. A night-light radiated from the hall to guide the way. As he walked through the living room, he noticed Dominique was asleep on the couch. He tiptoed to her, knelt, and kissed her forehead.

She awoke. "Everything okay?" She looked into his glowing green eyes.

"Everything's great!" He sat down as she sat up. "It was my dad who was activating and controlling things."

"Yes, that explains my misadventure. He never did like me."

"He wanted me to save my sister." He seemed to choke on his words. "I also met my birth mother."

"Awesome. Tell me more."

"Well, I was born at Fort Yates on the Standing Rock Indian Reservation. I'm the older twin. My great, great, great grandfather," he boasted, "knew Sitting Bull. He smoked the peace pipe with him."

"That's cool."

"Yes, it is and we can keep the mirror—it's now powerless because my dad has moved on."

She was quiet as she thought and smoked on her tobacco stick. "You know we're gonna have to hire a landscaper now for the backyard."

TWENTY-FIVE

A CHRISTMAS SPECIAL

THE NOISE FROM the washing machine rattled through the spin cycle while Dominique stood in front of her full-length mahogany framed mirror, primping her hair and making sure her clothes matched.

Matt stepped into the laundry room and informed her Travis and Nathan were safely at school and that her car was warmed and ready. She was to drive herself to Spokane to be part of a group signing for regional authors during the holiday season.

Wrek was awake and babysitting Ian in the natatorium. Nick was still in bed.

After Dominique left, Matt went to his bedroom, closed the door, and took off his clothes. Wearing only his white underwear, he dug through the back of his bottom dresser drawer and retrieved a rare purchase. He pulled from a brown paper sack, a buckskin skirt, an ornamental headdress, and a rattle. He felt proud to be of the Indian heritage as he eyed the items.

He wrapped the cloth around his waist and tied the string. He walked into the master bathroom, stood in front of the sink mirror, and fitted his feathered wear onto his head. He then took hold of Dominique's black eyeliner and drew thick lines upon his face.

Matt returned to the bedroom and inserted a tape into the cassette player. As the beating of the drum ushered in the music, he shook his Gourd rattle and lifted his legs. He danced around in circular motions, similar to what he had seen on television, trying to get a sense of how his ancestors commemorated their beliefs and ceremonialized their rituals.

After two songs, he was tired. While the tape continued to play, he sat on the carpet and loaded his pipe.

It was nearing six o'clock in the evening and the boys were wondering where their mother was since she hadn't come home from Spokane yet.

"Her book signing got over with at two," Wrek stated from the bay window in the living room as he looked out.

"She probably went shopping."

"I hope she went Christmas shopping!" Ian blurted with joy.

"Well, I know we're all hungry." Wrek turned to Matt. "I'll order the pizza if you pay for it."

After the Italian specialty was delivered and half eaten, Dominique arrived home. She entered the house with an armful of groceries. She requested help for the rest of the goods, but told everyone to stay out of the trunk.

"Why Mamma? Did you buy presents for us?" Ian's eyes widened as he waited for her answer.

While the family watched, she looked at him with a smile. "Maybe."

His face emitted a grin as he clapped and jumped.

In the kitchen, Dominique sat at the table and smoked a bowl while Wrek put the food away. "I've made a decision," she told Matt who was sitting beside her. "When my contract with Dorothy Lee ends next month, I'm going to let her go and just work directly with the publisher."

"Is that smart letting your agent go?"

"Sure. A lot of authors do it."

Ian went to bed early. Dominique kissed him good night after prayers then headed for the door.

"Mom?" he breathed quietly. "I have to tell you something."

She stopped and turned back. "What is it my Baby Zebra?" she asked him as she knelt beside his bed.

"I saw an Indian today."

"Yea?"

"I was peeking in your room and he was sleeping on your bed."

That's odd, she thought with confusion written upon her face. "How do you know he was an Indian?"

"He was wearing feathers on his head."

"Thank you for telling me. I'll check into it." She again kissed him upon his forehead and left his bedroom. "An Indian, huh?" she wondered as she walked through the hallway towards her bedroom, then entered in.

Dominique took a bath and after she wrapped the towel around her wet nude body, Matt came in. She was curious to see if he'd reveal anything. "So . . . what did YOU do today?"

"Nothing much." He preceeded to pee.

She returned to the bedroom and sat on her antique couch.

Matt stepped into the bedroom and saw the glare his wife wore. "What?" he asked in an innocent manner.

"I heard there was an Indian laying on our bed this morning?"

"Somebody has a mouth." After he confessed, Dominique insisted he wear his outfit for her and soon they were engaged in sexual activity.

The next morning, Travis and Nathan awoke with adventure on their minds. "We're not grounded anymore, we should go visit our cousins Chris and Sean."

"We could ask mom. She'll probably let us go through the mirror."

The two lads went down the staircase and headed to the kitchen where Dominique was making and baking.

"The mirror is powerless," she told them. "It won't take you anywhere."

"That sux, no more adventures."

"You don't need to go visiting anyways, we're gonna go get the tree soon and decorate things." She placed two pans with raw cinnamon dough into the oven.

"Awesome—I'm there!" Travis replied.

It was mid afternoon. Wrek and Nick set up the tree and strung the lights. Dominique had Christmas music playing from her stereo while she and Ian came across the glittery red and blue ornaments.

"Here's the gold and silver ones," Nathan spoke as he pulled the small boxes from the large storage container.

Ian hung the red bulbs and Travis the blue. Nick and Wrek tacked up silver trimming throughout the living room while Dominique fastened the stockings to the staircase rail, then fetched from the kitchen, candy canes for the tree. "I bought some cute ornaments yesterday," she spoke as she returned into the room and dangled a three inch reindeer from her fingers.

"Santa's reindeers!" Ian exclaimed.

"Do you have all eight of them?" Nick asked.

She nodded.

"Dasher, Dancer, Prancer, Vixon," the boys harmonized in a merry fashion, "Comet, Cupid, Donner, and Blitzen."

"What about Rudolph?" Ian blurted before they could sing any further.

"I have Rudolph." Dominique took hold of the one with the red nose and handed it to him.

"He's my favorite." He gave the ornament a little kiss as he carried it to the tree.

Dominique glanced at the time as she arose out of bed. "Three o'clock," she moaned, then lit a cigarette and tiptoed through the dark toward her bedroom door. She walked the hall and when she arrived into the living room, she noticed the tree lights were still on. As she stepped closer to the glow, she heard a snort. She turned and advanced to the couch where she observed Nathan sleeping. On the floor next to him, was his largest gift. It was as though the gift was his best friend spending the night. He had one end of it propped up on a pillow with the rest of it covered with a blanket. She went and retrieved her camera.

Sunday evening entered into existence with a light snowfall. Matt, Dominique, and the family freshened up and dressed themselves in nice clothes. They were on their way to the Christmas program at their church.

Nick was grumpy. He didn't want to go.

"Why not?" Ian made an earnest request of to his oldest brother. "Jesus being born is what Christmas is all about."

"And why," Dominique stepped in to quiz Ian, "was He born?"

"To die for us," he replied, "after he grew up."

"Why did he die for us?"

"To take away our sins and when we ask him to forgive us and live in our hearts, we will be saved."

"Saved from what?"

Nathan poked his head into the conversation. "From hell," he replied with a devilish voice.

"Who says?"

"God says in the Bible." Ian slipped on his jacket, Dominique zipped it, and they left the house.

It was a few days later when Dominique and her family were once again leaving for a Christmas function. This time, she let Nick stay home. They left the house and Matt drove them to the middle school.

While Travis joined his peers in the band room, his family went to the gym and sat themselves onto the cold steel bleachers. The crowded expanse was filled with chatter as they waited for the concert to start. Dominique looked over the leaflet and found that Travis' name was placed under the

percussion section as the number one chair. Her heart went
proud.

During the next forty-five minutes, she sat restless, eager
to hear her son play. After the intermediate band was finished
playing their array of songs and made their exit, the honor
band entered and took their places on the floor.

Soon the final strain was upon them; an advanced
version of Jingle Bells. As Travis pounded sixteenth notes and
flams with his drumsticks onto the snare and periodically
tapping the cymbal, chills ran up and down Dominique's
spine, giving her goosebumps throughout her small body.
She was almost in tears from the thumping of his drum.
She had played the snare drum when she was in the seventh
grade, but never advanced to the set. Her boy was now
fulfilling one of her dreams.

"This puts me in the mood for more Christmas stuff,"
Wrek admitted to his sister while they walked outside to her
car. "I have an idea."

Christmas Eve had arrived. All the stores were closed
for the holiday and the sun was arest for the night. The
lights on the tree were all aglow and the younger boys were
counting down the hours as they watched Christmas specials
on the television. Dominique had the turkey thawing on
the counter while she attended to the sugar cookies that Ian
insisted on leaving for his midnight visitor.

The clock struck ten. "It's bedtime!" Dominique called
out.

"Can I sleep on the couch?" Ian asked while his brothers
retired to doing whatever in their bedrooms. "I wanna see
Santa."

"No. He'll see you and leave. You don't want that, do
you?" she teased in a serious manner.

Ian dashed to the bathroom to brush his teeth.

She stepped to Wrek. "I'm putting him to bed now," she
whispered. "Wait about ten minutes, then do it."

With the lights off, Ian sat on his bed and said his prayers while his mom listened. When he was done, he laid back and Dominique brought the blankets up to his shoulders.

THUMP, THUMP, THUMP.

"What's that noise?" she mumbled, trying to curb her enthusiasm. It was quiet as she and Ian listened.

THUMP, THUMP.

They looked upwards at the ceiling.

"It's Santa Clause!" Ian roared as he sat up. "He's early and he probably brought Rudolph."

"Shh! You have to be quiet."

They arose to their feet and tiptoed across the room. They crept through the dark hallway until they reached the skirt of the living room. There, standing beside the lighted tree, was Ian's midnight visitor dressed in his furry red suit. He was pulling a gift from his bag while he breathed his ho ho ho.

Wrek chuckled to himself when he saw, from the nook of his eye, Ian and Dominique peeking around the corner. He set the gift down and proceeded to grab another.

Dominique tugged on Ian's arm, directing him back to his beroom.

"I saw Santa Clause!" Ian bragged in a low voice.

The next morning after Ian awoke, he jumped out of bed and dashed to the living room. He saw the assortment of gifts that extended out from underneath the Christmas tree. "Wow!" He cast his eyes to the stockings, then to the plate he left on the coffe table. "He ate them!"

"I ate them," his brother said from the third step of the staircase.

Ian glared at Nathan. "Santa did!"

Dominique entered the room. "That's enough Nathan." She winked at him.

Soon the family was opening gifts. Ian opened the blue one he saw Santa set down. "It's an ugly shirt!" he complained with a sour face as he held it up for his mom to see.

"It's a Hawaiian shirt. We're going to Hawaii tomorrow. Santa left us plane tickets."

"Awesome!" Travis and Nathan shouted together.

"I'm gonna go get leyed!" Nick gloated.

"Ha ha!" Dominique mocked his remark. "And when we get home, Uncle Wrek is moving to Pasco."

THE END!